THE
DEMON
GUARDIAN

THE DEMON GUARDIAN

Neil Davies

A
Grinning Skull Press
Publication

The Demon Guardian
Copyright © 2017 Neil Davies

The Skull logo with stylized lettering was created for Grinning Skull Press by Dan Moran, http://dan-moran-art.com/.
Cover designed by Jeffrey Kosh, http://jeffreykosh.wix.com/ jeffreykoshgraphics.

ISBN: 1-947227-00-9 (paperback)
ISBN-13: 978-1-947227-00-2 (paperback)
ISBN: 978-1-947227-01-9 (e-book)

DEDICATION

For Cathy, Jonathan, and Rhianne.

CONTENTS

PART I
SWANHILD

CHAPTER ONE

It was one of those rare mornings when Dennis Parkes woke at peace. Cautiously, he lifted his head, waiting for the quick, shadowy movements seen from the corner of his eye, the sibilant whispering filling the stale air of the small bedroom. There was nothing. Just still, silent darkness.

He thought of waking his wife, Swan, to share his sense of relief and happiness, but she had never heard the voices or seen the shadows move. If he woke her, she would be angry at being disturbed more than an hour before the alarm was due. It would ruin his mood. It would ruin the stillness. He eased his head back onto the pillow and lay awake, enjoying the silence, the peace.

Slowly, dawn lit up the window through the thin curtains, and birdsong twittered and whistled through the trees of nearby Ottmor Wood. If only all mornings could be like this, he would not need the medication, the therapy. It might even make his life with Swan less combative.

If only.

Wyatt Road lay quiet and sleepy on the outskirts of Anbal, a small village on the Wirral Peninsula. The commuter traffic, from Liverpool to the north and Chester to the south, bypassed Anbal on the M53 motorway. What little diverted through the narrow main street of the village itself passed the end of Wyatt Road without any thought of turning in. Wyatt Road was a dead-end. If you didn't live there and were not visiting, your only destination would be the turning circle just before the wooden stile leading to Ottmor Wood.

It was the quiet, more than anything, that had drawn Swanhild Parkes to number 20 when it came up for sale. A narrow mid-terraced house, it stood more or less equidistant between the end of the road and the wood. Built in the early 1930s, it had more-recent additions of a concrete driveway at the front, newly installed plumbing and electrics, and a narrow, but long, well-groomed garden at the back. That was eleven years ago, when she had persuaded Dennis that this should be their first family home. Now, standing at the kitchen sink, staring at the overgrown lawn, the legs of upturned plastic chairs like skeletal limbs reaching up from the long grass, she felt nothing but despair.

"It's not my fault I got made redundant," shouted Dennis from somewhere behind her. She had almost forgotten they were mid-argument. The same argument they had had almost weekly for the last three years.

"No," she said, agreeing. "But it is your fault that

the grass hasn't been cut for weeks."

"You know it hurts my back."

"We can't afford to get someone in anymore," she said, striving to be both truthful and understanding. "Since you can't do it, *I'll* have to do it at the weekend."

"I'll worry if you do that. I don't want you to do that."

His voice almost whined. She hated it when he whined.

"Yes, well, there's not much choice, is there?" She turned from the sink to face her husband. "Now, I have to get to work."

"I'll move the car," said Dennis. "May as well go to the shop while I'm out."

He turned and began burrowing through the accumulated clutter under the stairs for his shoes.

Swan wanted to be even more truthful. She wanted to tell her husband that he was a morbidly obese, out-of-work man in his early forties, and that it was no wonder his back and joints hurt, given the weight they were carrying. But she knew the redundancy had hurt him badly, destroyed his confidence, shoved him into depression, and that the weight gain was almost completely due to emotional eating since then. He was not currently fit for work, mentally or physically. She wanted to tell him these things, but she knew it would just deepen his depression and worsen an already terrible self-image. He needed to know she supported him, still loved him, despite all that had happened.

Dennis had found his shoes and, with some difficulty, put them on. Breathing heavily, he led the way out of the front door. Swan shrugged on her one and only coat and followed.

Dennis reversed his old Peugeot 405 out of the narrow driveway and waited, the engine idling. He felt comfortable in the car, able to relax, away from whispered voices, away from Swan. Alone. It had been bought for the long drive to his last place of work, and he held on to it stubbornly after the redundancy. Big and impractical it might be, given how little driving he now did, but it was *his*. And it was the only thing that connected him to his old life. His purposeful, *employed* life. When he hadn't felt quite so worthless. When he didn't spend days in introspection and deepening depresssion. When he felt confident his wife loved him.

Swan's Vauxhall Corsa reversed out, and the bright pink of the bodywork pulled a slight smile out of his frown. Even she agreed she bought it more for the colour than the car itself.

They waved to each other as she drove off, and Dennis waited until he saw her safely negotiate the junction at the end of the road before he put the Peugeot into gear and headed for the shops.

Just get the essentials and back home.

But did he really want to be home? There was nothing there but an empty house, another long day of watching the clock ticking slowly by, the flash of movement from the corner of his eye—and the voices.

He wanted to tell Swan, he really did. But how do you tell your wife that you hear voices in the home you share? She already thought him fat and useless, blamed him for his depression and for failing to get another job. To admit to hearing voices and seeing things would finally convince her he was completely insane. She would probably leave. He couldn't risk that.

Only two other people knew about the voices and the shadows: his local general practitioner, Dr. Banks, and his one and only friend, Travis Newman. The only two people he had told differed in their reactions.

"It's not that unusual," Dr. Banks had said. "Particularly in someone suffering from clinical depression, like yourself."

"But what do the voices mean?" said Dennis. "Why are they mostly unintelligible? Shouldn't they be sending me messages from God or something?"

Dr. Banks smiled. "The mind is a complex thing," he said. "It can push bad and unpleasant thoughts aside if it doesn't want to deal with them. It separates them, and they become a different part of you."

"You mean like another person in my head?"

"Not quite, but another aspect of you, certainly." Dr. Banks removed his narrow-framed glasses and held them in his right hand, twisting them back and forth as he spoke. "These are things you don't want to have to cope with just now, so they're pushed into the background. And mostly, that's where they stay. But every now and then they push back, and that's where the voices are coming from."

"So it's all in my mind," said Dennis. "Does this mean I'm psychotic or something?"

Dr. Banks shook his head. "No. It's not any kind of psychosis. It's *dissociation*. Like I said, it's quite common among those suffering from depression."

Travis, on the other hand, saw things slightly differently.

"So, you hear voices. Are they always in your head, or sometimes from outside?"

They had been sitting in their local Sainsburys cafe, meeting up during Travis's lunch break from his nearby office job, and before Dennis went shopping. Talking with Travis boosted Dennis's self-confidence enough to make it round the aisles without panicking.

"Sometimes in my head, sometimes not," said Dennis, keeping his voice low. He was sure some of the old people at neighbouring tables were listening.

"I don't reckon it's anything to do with depression," said Travis, casually dismissing what Dennis had told him about the doctor's opinion. "I think it's a lot simpler than all that stuff."

"Oh yes?" said Dennis, doubtfully. As a general rule, he sided with doctors over laymen, but he always had time for Travis's thoughts on matters, however outrageous they might turn out to be. "And so what do you think it is?"

"Simple." Travis leaned closer, lowering his voice to a whisper. "Your house is *haunted*."

Dennis managed to delay returning to the house for just over an hour, driving around, listening to the inane presenters on the equally inane radio shows. But he could not put if off forever. There were things he should be doing in the house.

He knew that Swan was right when she accused him of not doing enough. But most times, including today, the low moods and aching joints were just too much to handle, and certainly too much to allow for easy housework. Nevertheless, in an attempt to make Swan happy when she came home from work, he was determined to try.

I need to start pushing myself, he thought. *It's only fair to Swan. She's out earning the money. I have to do something here in the house so she knows I'm trying to help.*

If fear of the voices was a factor, it was one he kept deliberately in the background. Maybe, for once, if he didn't think about them, they might not be there. The quiet morning might extend into a quiet day.

Everything looked fine as he stopped in the driveway and climbed out of the car, something that was becoming increasingly difficult and painful as time went by. Even as he entered the house itself, the atmosphere was peaceful, totally lacking in the low susurration of voices he dreaded. At times like this, he could almost believe he imagined it all.

What definitely wasn't his imagination, however, was the musty, unclean smell. The smell of unwashed clothes and dusty furniture. Of carpets that hadn't been vacuumed. A smell that reminded him of old people, living on their own with no family to help. Old people who did not wash, could not clean, and wore the same clothes they had worn for the last who-knew-how-many days. It was not a smell that should exist in a house occupied by a couple in their forties. It was a smell that said no one cleaned. And that no one was him.

"Okay," he said, hanging up his fleece under the stairs. "First job of the day decided. Get rid of the smell."

He was an hour into it, wiping down the kitchen worktops and almost ready to vacuum the front room carpet when the first whispers slithered into the still, musty air.

He froze, a bottle of cleaning spray raised in one hand, the other grasping a wet paper towel, mid-wipe. The usual, sensible list ran quickly through his mind: plumbing; someone walking by outside; a nearby radio; the wind, even though there was none that day. He considered them all and discarded them. Neither was it coming from within his head. It was a voice, and the source was somewhere in the house.

He was long past the point of running from this thing. Frightened, yes, but not enough to run. As scary as they were, they had never hurt him. The voices in the house were always soft, on the edge of hearing, and always unintelligible. The movements were quick but nonthreatening, and never anywhere but in his peripheral vision. If he had to give a name to his feelings when that first voice hissed by, it would be disappointment. Disappointment that a day that had started whisper-free had become like every other day.

The voice continued, a diatribe of unknown words, and Dennis wondered briefly where this particular one was coming from. The corner of some room? Behind a half-open door? The attic? Beneath the suspended flooring? From where he stood, it came from the hallway, and he glanced quickly around the kitchen door to see, with some relief, what he had expected. Nothing.

But the voice continued. Just the one. That, at least, was something to be grateful for.

He had restarted cleaning, choosing to ignore the interruption, when he heard the first intelligible thing ever to come from the voices in the house. It froze his heart.

"Swanhild."

There could be no mistaking the sound of his wife's name, dropped into the middle of the usual nonsense.

He stood still. He listened. It came again.

"Swanhild."

The voice stopped, suddenly and completely. No echo or reverberation of sound. Just his wife's name one more time, and then silence.

He put down the cleaning spray and the paper towel

and hurried out into the hall. Nothing. He stepped into the front room. It was quiet and empty. Struggling up the stairs gave out no other clues. He didn't know what he was looking for, but he wanted some explanation for hearing his wife's name. He felt the same as he had the very first time he'd heard the voices. Frightened, confused, and sick.

He was still upstairs in the bedroom when the voice began again, from downstairs. It repeated one word, over and over.

"Swanhild. Swanhild. Swanhild."

Other voices joined it, a rising mass of eerie sibilance, all repeating his wife's name, none of them in unison.

Moving as quickly as he could, almost in tears from a sense of helplessness, a feeling that he was somehow failing his wife, he went back down into the hallway. The hissing, serpent-like voices surrounded him. It was no longer a case of where they came from. They came from everywhere, even from inside his own head. Repeated and repeated, battering him unceasingly, until the name became an almost unrecognisable collection of sounds. He pressed his hands to his ears. His mouth opened, wanting to shout, to tell them all to go away, but no sound emerged. Tears squeezed from tightly shut eyes.

Perhaps I really am insane.

The voices stopped with just as much suddenness as the one voice had earlier.

The silence had a sound of its own. A background hum of nothingness.

He opened his eyes. There was movement in the corners, shadows shifting and darting. It seemed somehow more frantic than usual. And then, not on the periphery, but directly in front of him, an intense Stygian blackness bled outward from the wall. It coalesced, grew, all but blocking the kitchen door from his sight. It radiated emptiness. A hole in the air before him.

Eyes snapped open in its depths. Veined, hungry, *lustful* eyes, blazing with an internal fire, shocking in their contrast with the void they floated in.

Terror gripped Dennis's heart, and he ran, puffing and panting, from the house.

CHAPTER TWO

"Thank God you're here," said Dennis as Travis's car drew to a stop at the end of the driveway.

"I told work it was a family emergency," said Travis, stepping out. "To be honest, it wasn't clear from your call what was going on."

"It's the voices, the darkness," said Dennis, pacing back and forth, agitated.

Travis saw the movement of curtains from several other houses. People were watching. Dennis's neighbours. No one had come out of their front doors to ask him what was wrong, but they were watching nonetheless.

"We need to get you inside," he said. "I'll make some tea, and we can talk about it."

He took Dennis gently by the shoulders and guided him towards the house.

He had known Dennis a long time. They had both been in their early twenties when they first met. Dennis was starting as a trainer in the small computer firm where Travis worked in marketing. They had quickly become friends through a shared appreciation of European horror movies and the kung fu films of Hong Kong. More importantly, he had the address of a mail order company that sold uncut versions on VHS. They had bonded immediately. When the computer firm folded, they lost touch, only to reconnect almost a year later, working for different companies out of the same multi-storey building on the outskirts of Manchester. It was a coincidence they took as fate, and they had never lost touch since. Not even as Travis continued into graphic design work with another company and Dennis moved to a local newspaper on the far side of Liverpool, managing their computers.

That was the company that had made Dennis redundant just over three years ago. Travis had watched his friend go downhill since.

As they neared the front door, Dennis resisted and pulled away. "No," he said. "Not until you know what's in there."

"You've told me all about the voices numerous times," said Travis. "And the things you see moving from the corner of your eye. What's so different this time?"

Dennis lowered his voice and leaned in towards Travis. There was a look of barely restrained panic in his eyes. "I saw something right in front of me. Not out the corner of my eye, but right in front," said Dennis. "And I know what they want. They want Swan!"

Swan stared blankly at her coffee. It swirled from the illicit spoonful of sugar she had stirred in just seconds before. Today she needed it sweet.

"Is it really that bad?" Piers Boyson stepped into the tiny kitchen, squeezing past Swan in a way that could have been awkward except for one thing. Piers's boyfriend would not be amused.

"Sometimes." Swan smiled. "How's Davin getting on in his new job?"

"Fine." Piers searched the cupboards for his box of Green Tea, finding it tucked away at the back. "And we can finally save for the wedding."

"I expect an invite."

"Of course."

As he waited for the kettle to boil, Piers looked to Swan, still staring morosely into her drink.

"Speaking of marriages," he said. "How's Dennis doing?"

Swan looked up and forced a smile. "Same as always."

"So, things not good between you two then?"

"Is it that obvious?" Swan sighed. "He just doesn't seem to try anymore. When we met, we seemed to enjoy the same kind of things, but now..."

"I'm sure he's finding the whole thing difficult, too," said Piers. "The redundancy hit both of you hard."

Swan nodded, never taking her eye off the coffee, the swirl gradually slowing until it slid to a graceful stop.

"I just get fed up sometimes," she said quietly. "I feel down."

Leaving his green tea to brew, Piers placed a gentle hand on Swan's shoulder.

"You should come out with Davin and me," he said. "Just for a few drinks after work. Something to take your mind off things for a while."

"That's kind of you, but I have to get straight home." Swan smiled again, slightly broader this time. "Some time soon though, yes?"

Piers's attention was drawn by a passing doctor. Tall, muscular, perfect hair and teeth. Almost a caricature of *the young doctor*. He even had the stethoscope around his neck.

"Doctor Mayson," whispered Piers. "Now there's something to take your mind off your troubles."

Swan glanced at the passing doctor and blushed. "I would never do that," she said.

Piers smiled. "I would."

"We should get back to work," said Swan, laughing, feeling better than she had. "There's probably patients waiting."

As they left the kitchen, Swan's eyes lingered on the retreating back of Dr. Mayson.

Dennis let Travis lead the way. He knew it was a cowardly thing to do, but he was too frightened of what he might see. It was all he could do to hide behind his friend and not run away again. He had not felt such fear since, as a small child, he would wake from nightmares, screaming and crying. Even then, his father told him he was a coward. Only his mother seemed sympathetic.

The child that never quite grew up inside him wished his mother were alive and with him now.

"What am I meant to be looking for exactly?" said Travis as he opened the door and stepped into the hallway. "Oh my God!"

"What?" Dennis almost turned and fled, panic rising

within. "What do you see? What's there?"

"Your house is such a mess!" said Travis, turning and grinning.

Dennis almost punched him, only slowly seeing the funny side and forcing a smile. He should have known better than to think Travis could keep his sense of humour in check.

"There's nothing there, Dennis," said Travis seriously. "At least, nothing I can see out of the ordinary."

Dennis looked past his friend to see his hallway. It was as if nothing had happened.

"I saw something coming out of that wall," he said. "I know it sounds ridiculous, but I saw it."

"What did it look like?" Travis ran his fingers over the wall indicated by Dennis. It was solid. "Was it a person?"

"I...I don't know." Dennis pinched the bridge of his nose between thumb and forefinger. He could feel a headache growing. "It was just a shape. Black. And then the eyes."

"Eyes?"

"This pair of eyes opened up and looked at me from the blackness." Dennis sighed. "That's when I ran."

Travis placed a hand on Dennis's shoulder. "Don't worry about it, mate. If I'd seen that, I'd have run, too." He smiled. "Close the door and I'll make us a cup of tea."

Dennis watched Travis head into the kitchen, then, as suggested, turned to close the front door.

Did I really see that thing? Or am I truly going mad?

He was not sure how to answer. When he ran, he had no doubt about what he saw. Now, he wondered whether he had overreacted to something that might have a perfectly reasonable explanation. Not that he could think of one at that moment.

As he turned to follow Travis into the kitchen, the house breathed out in one long breath.

"Sssswwwwaaaannnnhhiilllllddd."

Swan's right leg was hooked over the back of the driver's seat. Her left foot brushed the low roof with each thrust, her lover's arm hooked behind the knee, keeping it high. At first, she wondered how he could be in any way comfortable, squeezed between the front seats and the back. But then he began to move, and she no longer cared. He kissed her mouth, her cheek, her neck. Breathed heavily into her tangled hair. Lifted himself up on muscular arms and looked down on her nakedness, smiling, sweating.

She had no idea how he was at medicine, but there was no doubting that Dr. Mayson was a good fuck.

CHAPTER THREE

The world through the windscreen melted as heavy raindrops distorted Swan's vision.

What have I just done?

She sat alone in her car. Dr. Mayson—she didn't even know his first name—had not long driven off home. Back to his wife and children. She knew he had children because afterwards he had shown her their pictures. Jen and Simon. He told her his children's names, but never his own. What kind of screwed morality was that?

Not that I'm in any position to comment on another's morality.

She could smell the sex they'd had. It tainted the air. Rain spat in her face as she let down the driver's window. It speckled the plastic of the dashboard, but at least it cleared the air a little.

I suppose I should be grateful he had condoms with him.

But then again...

He had condoms with him! Guess I'm not the first.

The dashboard clock, lending a spectral light to a rapidly darkening interior, told its own story of her infidelity. As did her iPhone, which was in her bag and turned off. The phone she could explain, using the poor-to-no reception in the hospital as an excuse for being out of touch. But the time… Almost an hour and a half late. Dennis would not be happy.

Dennis!

The first tears came slowly, meandering over her cheeks with the slightest of tickling sensations.

Trying to understand why she'd done it seemed a fruitless expenditure of energy. Words like *urge*, *uncontrollable*, and *desperate* were trivial and incomplete. It had been a *collection* of urges. She *had* been out of control. And she and Dennis had hardly been intimate since Dennis's self-image worsened almost two years ago. But it was more than that. She had felt not only out of control, but out of her body. Pushed aside by *something*. And it was that *something* that had followed Dr. Mayson to this secluded spot. That *something* that engaged energetically in quick, almost violent, sex with a near stranger in the back of her car.

She started the engine. There seemed little point in analysing further. It was the first time she had been unfaithful to Dennis. But she could not rid herself of the feeling that it might not be the last. The *something* could return at any time, and that thought brought both excitement and sickness to her stomach.

Windscreen wipers restored solidity to the world outside as she drove off, leaving the driver's window down, the rain mixing with her tears.

"Where is she?"

Dennis sat forward in his armchair, eyes flitting between the clock, Travis relaxing on the couch, and SpongeBob on the TV. Travis had chosen the channel. It was something that would normally make both of them laugh. Dennis did not feel like laughing today.

"She'll be along soon," said Travis, smiling at the TV. "Just try and relax. Watch some SpongeBob. Personally, I find I empathise more with Patrick. What do you think?"

Dennis, not even conscious of the attempt to draw him into light-hearted conversation, looked again at the clock.

"Even working late, she'd normally be home by now. Do you think she's okay?"

"She's fine," said Travis, struggling to keep the smile on his face. He saw his role, for now, as keeping Dennis on the right side of sanity until Swan got home. He just hoped *she* could do a better job than he was doing.

"What if the voices start again?" said Dennis, gently rocking back and forth. "What if that thing comes back out of the wall? What if she's been in some kind of accident?"

The changes in the focus of Dennis's anxiety almost caught Travis out. When Dennis started on about the voices or the manifestation he was convinced he'd experienced, Travis more or less switched off. There was nothing he could say. But worrying about Swan being in an accident was something he could not ignore. That was a *real* worry, and one that had crossed his mind, too. Not that he would ever admit that to Dennis.

"She hasn't been in any accident," he said, hoping he sounded convincing. "She's just late. We've all been late in our time. Even you, Dennis."

Dennis said nothing, but his silence was tense as he clenched and unclenched his fists, rocking back and forth on the edge of the chair.

When they heard the key turn in the front door, it was difficult to say which of them was more relieved.

Swan perched on the edge of Dennis's chair. He grasped her hand in his fist, unwilling to let go.

"Why didn't you tell me about the voices, Dennis?" She wanted desperately to go upstairs and change, have a shower, wash away every trace of Dr. Mayson, but Dennis would not let her out of his sight.

"I was worried you'd think I'd finally cracked," said Dennis, smiling up at her nervously. "I thought with Dr. Banks's help, and Travis's, I'd get it sorted out without you ever having to know."

"And *you* didn't think to tell me?" This was directed at Travis, who still sat across the room.

"Dennis didn't want me to."

Swan shifted slightly on the arm of the chair. She was conscious of the way her skirt rode up above her knees. She kept her legs very deliberately pressed together. It was not that she was shy around Travis, but she hadn't wanted to put her panties back on after using them to wipe herself in the car earlier. She had discarded them in a ditch near the site of her liaison with Dr. Mayson.

"I've known you almost as long as I've known Dennis," she said. "You should have told me."

"It was different this time, Swan," said Travis. "Dennis has never called me out of work before, not because of the voices. He was genuinely terrified of coming back into the house alone."

She tightened her grip on Dennis's hand.

"I'd never seen anything right in front of me before," said Dennis quietly.

"It must have been scary," said Swan. "You did the right thing, calling Travis."

"I would have called you, but I know your phone doesn't work well in the hospital. And you couldn't just leave patients sitting there, waiting to see you."

"Maybe it's stress?" said Swan. "Between how depressed you are, then hearing the voices again. Things can get confused with shadows, light, even cars passing outside the window."

"Maybe," said Dennis, but it was obvious to Swan that he did not believe that. If *she* had seen it, she probably wouldn't believe all the usual, rational explanations either.

"There is one other thing," said Dennis. "I wasn't sure whether to tell you."

"Tell me, Dennis," said Swan. "Really, you can tell me anything. You know that."

With only a slight hesitation, Dennis continued. "After Travis was here and we came back inside, I heard the voices again."

Swan smiled. "Well, I don't suppose they're just going to disappear like that, even with someone else in the house."

"No, it's not that," said Dennis. "It's what they said. What they were saying before the thing appeared. Normally I can't make it out, but this time they were saying your name. Swanhild."

"*My* name?"

"Very clearly. They kept saying your name, over

and over."

Swan said nothing, a sudden tightening of her stomach making her feel sick. She had no proof, but she felt strangely certain that Dennis was hearing these voices at the same time she was with Dr. Mayson. She didn't believe in ghosts and all that supernatural crap, but she did wonder if Dennis's subconscious somehow knew what she was doing. Telepathy and such had been investigated by science, hadn't it? Weren't there some scientists who claimed it was real? Hadn't the Americans done something with it during the war, or the Cold War, or whenever? She didn't believe in ghosts, but she was willing to believe in the untapped power of the human mind.

If Dennis's subconscious knew what I was doing, how long before it gets to his conscious thoughts? Was it worth risking my marriage for one vaguely disappointing fuck? Why did I do it?

She became slowly aware that Travis was staring at her oddly. Was that suspicion on his face? Had he somehow guessed?

Following Dennis's revelation, one of her legs had unconsciously slipped from the arm of the chair. Her thighs had parted and her skirt ridden higher. With sudden embarrassment, she rectified the situation, but was it too late? Was that why Travis was looking at her so strangely?

She needed a change of clothes. She needed a shower. Most of all, she needed to throw up to try and ease the churning of her insides.

CHAP+ER F⊕UR

Travis Newman had poured himself a vodka and topped it with lime cordial almost before the door to his apartment clicked shut. He needed a drink.

His party trick, in his younger, wilder days, had been to drink vodka straight from the bottle. Over the years he had softened it with various mixers, settling finally on lime. It helped to lessen the numbing effect. Dennis had been his almost-constant sidekick at those parties, perhaps never quite matching him drink for drink, but making a good effort. It reminded him of just how long he had known Dennis, and of the fun, and sometimes risky, times they'd shared. All long before Swan appeared, of course.

He shrugged off his coat, let it fall across the back of the apartment's one armchair, and carried his drink to the small dining table, set under the window overlooking Rose Park. A large part of his monthly salary went on rent, but it was worth it to have this prime location in the new apartment block, built just ten years ago on the outskirts of Anbal. Before moving, he had lived in a one-room bedsit in Oxton, with no window at all. This three-room apartment, with a view over the flowered borders and well-kept grass of the park, was a luxury he felt he deserved.

He had moved back to Anbal just after Dennis and Swan bought their house.

Swan. What to do about Swan?

He sat in one of the two dining chairs and placed his elbows on the table to either side of his drink.

How certain am I of what I think I saw? Certain enough to risk ruining my best friend's marriage?

He was not in the habit of looking at Swan's legs, as nice as they were. Just doing that felt too much like he was betraying his friend. But the movement of her leg sliding off the arm had caught his eye, and he had looked automatically.

It sparked a memory of that scene from *Fatal Attraction.*

She had not been wearing any underwear. He was *almost* certain.

The shame he felt that his immediate reaction had been arousal was largely overpowered by the disturbing thoughts on *why* she wasn't wearing any. None of them looked good for Dennis.

"What do I do?" he said to his drink, before lifting it and downing it in one. "The last thing Dennis needs at the moment is me telling him his wife is being unfaithful. But I can't stand by and watch him being played for a fool, either."

Why now, Swan? Why did you have to go and fuck things up now?

The temptation of another drink was strong, but

he knew himself well enough to know that the second drink would lead to a third, then a fourth, until he drank himself stupid. That did not seem like a good idea at present. He needed a clear head to think.

A faint sibilance in the air was suggestive of a whisper, and Travis looked out the window, wondering if it had come from someone in the park. There was no one there.

"This business with Dennis and the voices is getting to me," he said, smiling. "Get a grip, Travis."

He even knew the term for what he had just heard, thanks to many hours watching various ghost hunter-style reality shows on TV. *Audio pareidolia.* Hearing words in sound when they're not actually there.

It really didn't help, however, that the word he had heard, quite clearly, if softly, was *Swanhild.*

He was more unnerved than he cared to admit. This was one of those times when he really needed some company.

"I can't believe you've never told us about this before," said Jake.

Jake Maxfield and Elton Hoggarth had arrived at Travis's door together. They smelt of beer. It was a fair bet they had been together at the pub when they got Travis's call. Now they sat on his small two-seater settee, Elton still wearing the woollen hat he rarely took off, cold cans of beer in their hands from Travis's fridge, hearing about Dennis's voices and the apparition for the first time.

"It was something Dennis told me in confidence," said Travis defensively. "I'm only telling you now because things seem to have escalated, and there are other issues, too."

"We've spent hours sitting here, watching *Most Haunted*, *Ghost Hunters*, *Ghost Adventures*, and the rest," said Elton, disbelief and alcohol evident in the high pitch of his voice. "And you don't tell us when something actually happens to one of our friends?"

"You two hardly know Dennis," said Travis.

"We've met him."

"The point is," said Jake, sounding slightly less drunk than Elton. "You've told us now. We should investigate."

"Do our own ghost hunt," said Elton, smiling, sounding excited.

"At the moment, I just want to talk things through," said Travis. "Let's not get ahead of ourselves. I just needed to share this, and I knew you two wouldn't immediately assume Dennis was nuts."

"Damn right," said Jake. "And what about these other issues you mentioned?"

Travis hesitated before coming to a decision. "I think I'll leave those until you're both sober."

CHAPTER FIVE

Dennis woke and automatically reached for his phone on the bedside table to shut off the alarm. Only when he picked it up did he realise it was still several hours before the alarm would go off. It was not an alarm that woke him. It was the whispering.

It filled the room. Although it had taken a moment for his tired, confused mind to register it, the hissing, slithering sibilance washed back and forth like waves on the shore. And like the waves, it threatened to overwhelm him, drown him in its relentless advance.

"Stop it!" He covered his ears with his hands, but it did no good. "Stop it! Shut up!" He was shouting and sobbing. Why wouldn't it go away? Why wouldn't it leave him alone? It was too much. He couldn't cope.

"What the fuck are you doing?" Swan, jerked awake by Dennis's shouting, sat up angrily. When she saw the tears, she softened, placing a hand on Dennis's arm soothingly. "What's wrong? Bad dream?"

"No," said Dennis, uncovering his ears as the whispering receded and turning to look at his wife. "Not a bad dream. Didn't you hear it? The voices? The whispering? It was so loud."

Swan shook her head and wished she could be more positive for him, but she also did not want to lie.

"I'm sorry," she said. "I didn't hear anything other than you shouting."

He let the sobbing subside before speaking, his voice under slightly more control than before. Nevertheless, there was a tremble in it that he could do nothing to stop.

"I don't understand what's happening," he said, wiping tears from his eyes. "I don't understand why nobody else hears them. There's so many, and so loud."

"Could you tell what they were saying?" Swan reached up and stroked her fingers down his tear-damp cheek. "Was it my name again?"

"No," said Dennis, forcing a slight smile. "I couldn't tell you what they were saying, but I know it wasn't your name this time."

The bedroom window smashed open with a sudden rush of wind, startling them both. Swan was the first to recover, and laugh nervously.

"Mustn't have been closed properly," she said, looking to Dennis for agreement. But Dennis was gripping his chest, trying to push the sudden tightness and pain away. His face was bathed in sweat. But even worse than the pain, when the wind burst into the bedroom through the window, it carried a voice with it. Not whispering, but deep and clear and angry. It said one word.

"*Swanhild!*"

Dennis did not remember much about the ambulance ride. He knew they'd hooked him up to a machine in the back of it, checking his heart. He knew they'd given him some kind of painkiller, which had made no difference to the pain at all. Then he heard the siren...

...and remembered nothing until the doors swung open and he was put into a wheelchair and taken inside the hospital.

He was reasonably certain Swan was there, holding his hand for the majority of the journey, and the wheelchair ride into A&E. He was glad she was there. He felt safer with her there.

Is this what a heart attack feels like? Am I dying?

It felt as though his chest was being crushed by an elephant.

He was wheeled into a curtained cubicle and transferred to an A&E trolley-bed, where they inserted a cannula into his arm and began feeding morphine to him. He remembered that. It was the first time the pain began to ease, just slightly. When, after a few frantic questions—answered by Swan—and blood being taken, they asked him how the pain was now, he told them. They increased the morphine. Then, finally, the pain faded.

At some point, time seeming irrelevant to Dennis, he was wheeled through to an assessment area, where it was thankfully quieter than the constant hustle and noise of A&E. Here they did more tests and took more blood, while Dennis lay quietly, uncaring as long as the pain did not return. He thought Swan looked concerned, worried, and felt strangely pleased about that. Not because she was worried, but because it showed she cared. Sometimes he doubted it. Usually when he looked in a mirror, or actually thought about what he had become.

"We don't think it was a heart attack."

Those were the first words he remembered taking note of when he looked back later. In some strange way, he felt more disappointed than relieved. It was not that he wanted a heart attack, as much as hoping it was something serious enough to cause people to care for him more. He knew there was little logic in the thought. Perhaps it was even a little pitiful. But he was disappointed for himself, and faintly embarrassed at having wasted everyone's time and worry. Now they would despise him more. He couldn't even have a decent medical condition!

"We won't be one-hundred percent certain until the blood work comes back, but we're as certain as we can be at the moment," said the doctor, continuing over Dennis's despondency. "Nevertheless, we'd like to keep you overnight for observation, and to give a chance for the test results to get to us."

It took Dennis a moment to realise that people, medical and Swan, were waiting for some kind of response from him. He managed a nod, and a mumbled, "Fine," and they seemed happy.

Later, he was wheeled through to the cardiac ward. Swan had kissed him and left just before the move. There seemed little point in her coming up to the ward and hanging around any longer. After all, he hadn't even had a heart attack!

The ward was noisier than the assessment area, and the staff was less friendly. The first thing they did was take his blood pressure, and then more blood. He could already tell it was going to be a long day, and a longer night.

CHAP+ER SIX

Jake and Elton climbed the stile at the end of Wyatt Road and walked into the shadowed darkness of Ottmor Wood. It was a place they often went, secluded, eerie, perfect for hiding from the rest of society and smoking some weed. Preferable to the small apartment the two of them shared with straight-laced office clerk Alison, Elton's older sister. She did not approve of their smoking of cannabis, and would certainly not allow it in the apartment. And it was not a smell that was quickly cleared from the air.

"Did you notice anything strange about Dennis's house on the way past?" said Elton, negotiating the small path that wound between trees, clumps of grass, and the perennial mud that lay just off the edge, waiting for the unwary foot.

"Nothing." Jake followed close behind, peering into the depths of the wood on either side, trusting Elton to lead him, without misstep, to their regular place.

"Didn't look like anyone was home."

The path, if followed without deviation, would bring them out on the main road into Anbal. Along the way, there were narrower paths jutting off to the fields that surrounded the woods on all other sides. Unless you had an unhealthy interest in cows, or lived on Wyatt Road, there were few reasons to enter the woods at all. Dog walkers were the most common transient visitors, and sometimes small groups of children, daring each other to do anything other than *run* through the *haunted* woods. Most forests and woods had legends and grim tales told about them, and Ottmor Wood was no different.

"Do you ever wonder if some of the stories are true?" said Elton as he led Jake off the main path. The tangled undergrowth moved disturbingly under his foot with each step. He knew it was just soft ground, but there were times when his imagination tried to convince him otherwise.

"You always ask that," said Jake, following. "If you believed all the stories, there'd hardly be anyone left in Anbal, and we'd be tripping over the decomposing bodies of the murdered and the suicides."

"Not if they all just disappeared, like Mister Jackson a few years back."

"The only person who's going to disappear is you if you don't shut up," said Jake, sighing. "And everyone knows Mister Jackson ran off with that woman who used to run the mobile library at the school, despite what Missus Jackson says."

They reached a small clearing, much of it trampled down by their own boots. On one side was the trunk of a fallen tree, supplying the perfect bench, or backrest for those who preferred to sit on the ground. Depending on who you spoke to, the tree had fallen after being hit by lightning, or been blown down by near-hurricane winds, or had just rotted. Jake and Elton didn't care about how it had fallen, only that it provided the perfect place for them to sit, relax, drink, and smoke.

Elton lit up, inhaled and passed the joint to Jake.

"What d'you make of all this stuff with Dennis?"

"I think we've finally got a haunted house to investigate." As Jake spoke, smoke curled out of his mouth and dissipated against the shadows thrown by the encircling trees. "Dennis never struck me as the kind to make things like this up. It sounds promising."

"Travis will talk Dennis round, I'm certain of it."

Elton took the joint back from Jake, and they fell silent for a moment, enjoying the soft breeze, the rustling of the woods, the weed.

"I've never noticed that before," said Elton, pointing to the far side of the clearing.

Jake looked and, at first, could see nothing. Then he noticed the rusty red showing through the mud and flattened grass.

He stood and walked over, hearing Elton following as he squatted and cautiously reached out fingers.

"What is it?" said Elton, standing a little back, just in case.

"Stone," said Jake, running his hand over the roughness. "Sandstone, to be precise. Like most of this area."

"Is that all," said Elton, obviously disappointed. "I thought we might have found something interesting."

"It *is* interesting," said Jake, exploring further with his hands. "For a start, how come we've never noticed it before. And it's too regular to just be the bedrock poking through. It feels as though it was shaped. Like a block, or a slab. And there's something carved on it."

Elton quickly got to his knees alongside Jake. "Carved? Like figures, or words, or what?"

"Help me clear the crap off it."

Using their hands, the joint hanging precariously from the corner of Elton's mouth, they cleared as much mud, grass, and roots away from the stone as they could. It became quickly obvious that it was a slab of sandstone, roughly rectangular.

"You know," said Elton. "It looks kind of like a gravestone."

"Thank you for putting that thought in my head," said Jake, smiling. "But you're right. Nothing else looks like a grave around it though. Probably just a coincidence."

"Probably," echoed Elton, but he wasn't convinced. In fact, he *wanted* it to be a gravestone. It made the find even more exciting and would add considerably to the legends of Ottmor Wood. And their own reputation locally.

"Feels like letters," said Jake, running his hands over the surface of the slab once more. "Too dark in here to see properly, but I can just about make things out by feeling."

A light flared as Elton sparked his lighter to life and held it towards the stone.

"Hold it lower," said Jake.

The carving became clearer, and they could make out some letters, even though much of the stone was badly weathered.

The breeze strengthened to a wind, moaning through the trees. The flame of Elton's lighter began to gutter. They both shivered with a sudden drop in temperature.

"First letter looks like a *G*, followed, maybe, by a *J*," said Jake, squinting as he tried to make out the faint lines of indentation.

"What kind of word starts with *G-J*?" said Elton.

"I think there's an *L* somewhere in there, maybe an *A*, or it could be an *N*?" Jake sat back on his haunches. "It's no good. Just can't make it out."

"You know what we should do?" said Elton. "We should tell someone who knows stuff. This shit could be ancient. Don't colleges and universities have whole departments to deal with this kind of shit?"

"Just occasionally you have a good idea," said Jake, nodding.

He pulled out his phone and took three pictures, each from a slightly different angle.

"We can email someone these images and see what they say."

The wind strengthened, the moaning turning into roaring. Elton's lighter blew out. Dead leaves and loose grit began to swirl into the air, blow in their faces.

"Is it just me, or is this getting strange?" said Elton, putting the lighter back into his pocket, followed quickly by the joint, snuffed out with his fingers.

"I think we should go home," said Jake. "This is not the weather to be in the woods."

They both hurried away from the clearing as the first drops of rain fell, heavy drops that splashed on their heads, clattered against the leaves on the trees. The growing storm followed them as they hurried back up Wyatt Road.

CHAP+ER SEVEN

Swan exited the hospital main entrance and stopped, breathing out a long, slow breath. She had been frightened, realising, in that moment, when she genuinely thought Dennis was having a heart attack, just how much she wanted him around. She had almost cried with relief when the doctor said it almost certainly *wasn't* a heart attack. She could barely hold back the tears now.

A quick check of her phone showed it had just gone on 1:00 pm. Time had not seemed an issue inside the hospital, with Dennis. She had not realised how long they had been there since the panicked emergency call that morning. Half the day gone. Fortunately, it wasn't one of her working days or she would have been in serious trouble. Her manager was not the most flexible or understanding of women.

The sudden *whoop* of an ambulance moving cars out of the way made her jump. She watched, with no real interest, as it reversed into one of the ambulance bays outside A&E. The crew wheeled an elderly lady out in a wheelchair, bringing back memories of when she and Dennis had arrived earlier. She looked away before it became impossible to hold back the tears that still threatened to pour from her eyes.

She forced herself to breathe slowly, deeply. Public displays of sadness were all too common on the hospital grounds, but she had no intention of adding to them.

Looking across the near-full car park at a steady line of hopeful drivers circling the bays, waiting to pounce, she realised that, travelling with Dennis in the back of the ambulance, she did not have her car with her. The bus shelters over the far side of the car park did not look particularly inviting, and neither did the thought of the bus journey itself. She would have to phone someone.

The first few spits of rain pricked her face as she looked up at the leaden sky. Heavy clouds were ready to unload, and a rising wind began to bite through her jeans, t-shirt, and thin raincoat. There had not been time to think about such inconsequential things as the weather, while dressing hurriedly and waiting for the ambulance to arrive.

She needed a lift home, and soon.

Piers would be at work, as would Travis. It was a little sad, she thought, that outside of work, or Dennis's friend, she had no one she could turn to at such a time. She might have to go to the phlebotomy office and wait until Piers could take a break.

She knew someone was looking at her. It was a strange sense of discomfort, of knowing she was being looked over, examined. It was not something she felt often. In truth, she was not sure she had ever felt it before. Certainly not this strong.

When she looked quickly around the constant traffic of people outside the hospital entrance, the man studying her was obvious. He was one of the many flouting the hospital's no smoking policy, and he had paused, the cigarette held close, but not between, his open lips, when she turned and looked straight at him.

Did she know him? She didn't think so. He was not familiar, other than the general familiarity of his look and dress. Unshaven, t-shirt, no jacket despite the weather, proudly displaying his sleeve of tattoos. Worn jeans, heavy work boots. A manual labourer perhaps, or one of the many unemployed in the area. She could not say which. But she was certain she didn't know him.

So why was he looking at her so blatantly? And why did she feel a thrill deep in her stomach—and lower.

The smell from the bins was bad, almost overwhelming. Swan had no idea what was in the black bags bulging out of the metal containers, but she was vaguely aware of just how close her face was being regularly, rhythmically pushed towards them with each sudden, hard thrust from behind. She didn't care.

Bent over the bins, jeans and panties around her knees, she grunted with each push of the stranger behind her. At least he had thrown his cigarette away.

Leading him around the side of the hospital to the rarely visited bin area had been exciting and a little frightening. She had not felt fully in control of her actions, just like with Dr. Mayson. When he turned her round and bent her over, she had smiled. It had not felt quite like her smile. When he threw her raincoat up her back and tugged her jeans and panties down, the rain began to fall; heavy droplets splashed on the bare skin of her bottom, making her laugh. Strangely, it did not sound like her laugh. When he forced himself deep inside her, unprotected, she had both cried and screamed. It hurt, but she was enjoying the hurt. Dennis was always gentle, loving. Right now she just wanted to be fucked.

The rain fell heavier, soaking her head, her hair, her bare thighs. She didn't care. The faint *splash* that accompanied each deep thrust was almost pleasing, oddly erotic.

When he orgasmed and pulled out, she was disappointed. She had got close, but not close enough. Rain mixed with the semen she felt leaking out. She would need another shower. But at least, now, she had a ride home.

CHAP+ER EIGH+

Simon Forrester, Professor of Archaeology, working out of Smithurst University in Taupington, Cheshire, looked at the clock hanging on the wall. Almost 4:00 pm. His lectures were over for the day and, as much as he might love his job, he was relieved. It had been a long day, with some awkward students and a mischievous overhead projector that insisted on flickering and dying at random intervals, only to start up again the moment Tech Support arrived. It had just been one of those days.

He gathered up his papers and his laptop. With a last, quick look around to ensure nothing obvious had been missed, he left the room, turning the lights off as he went.

It was still bright as he exited the building and joined students and other faculty members milling around Cloisters. With the usual lecture theatres taken, he had been pushed out to a windowless room in Tower Block. The Tower, like many of the other buildings on campus, was relatively new, having been part of the building spree following Smithurst's promotion from a college to a university two years ago. Unfortunately, also like many of the other buildings, the focus had been on quantity, not quality. Small, windowless rooms were not ideal for either the students or the lecturer. It had been a claustrophobic end to a stressful day.

He needed a coffee and a sit-down. Fortunately, the perfect place was on the ground floor of the same building that housed the Archaeology Department. Smiling and nodding to those students and faculty he knew, he walked quickly through the campus towards Weston.

The Brasserie, or Weston's Coffee Shop as it was more popularly known, sat on the ground floor of Weston Building. He ordered a latte, then found an empty table to sit at. The dim lighting eased his growing headache a little. On the walk, he had noted the storm clouds moving slowly closer, and he often seemed to get headaches when there was a storm about to break. He had never tried to understand it. He just accepted it.

Sipping at the latte, he opened up his laptop.

"Time to check on emails," he said quietly to himself, quickly looking around in case anyone else had heard him. The few students scattered about the room were too involved in their own thoughts and conversations to take any notice of a professor talking to himself. They probably considered it normal behaviour for an *old* professor anyway. Even though he had only just turned fifty, most students treated him, politely, as an old man.

"Spam, spam, spam," he said as he hit the delete button again and again. In his head, the *Monty Python* spam song had started, and he knew it would probably stay with him for the remainder of the day.

He bypassed a few official looking emails, deciding he could look at them later, and eventually highlighted the subject of *found a strange rock*. The sender was a *jmax*, who he had never heard of, and there were attachments. He was well trained to be wary of emails with attachments from strangers, but his curiosity won out. He would have to trust his computer's anti-virus software.

There was nothing malicious about the email, once opened. He read the brief message, but he was far more interested in the images of a regular-shaped sandstone rock that accompanied the email. One image, in particular, interested him. Taken from a low angle, it showed, quite clearly, the first few letters carved into the rock. *G-J-A-L-L*. There were more, but the image did not show them well enough to even guess at them. But, with a Ph.D. in Norse Mythology behind him, those letters, combined with the known Viking history of the area where the rock had been found, seemed very clearly Old Norse. He needed to see the rock in person.

He began to type his reply just as the storm broke overhead, a sudden explosion of thunder shaking the table and stabbing pain through his head. He'd known it was on its way. And it sounded like a bad one.

CHAPTER NINE

Travis was furious.

"My best friend has a possible heart attack, and you can't be bothered to call me?"

Swan had not long finished her shower, and was in her dressing gown, browsing on her phone, when the doorbell rang. Travis pushed his way in, angrily. She made no move to stop him.

"I only found out when you posted it to fucking Facebook!"

"I'm sorry," said Swan. "I wasn't thinking straight, okay?" She stood before him, uneasily aware of her nakedness beneath the dressing gown. She felt vulnerable, but not scared. She knew Travis would never hurt her, however angry he was. He was like Dennis in that way.

"I wouldn't expect you to call me when it happened, obviously," said Travis, his anger beginning to ease. "But once he was settled in the hospital, you could have let me know. At the very least, when you left to come home."

An ugly memory of bins, the stranger, the rough sex, and an uneasy drive flashed in her head, making her blush and feel faintly sick. She did not understand how she could have done that. Just as she could not understand what had happened with Dr. Mayson.

"I was confused," she said. "I honestly don't know what I was thinking about when I left the hospital." *Or what I was doing!* "Have you been to see him?"

"Just before I came here." Travis calmed down, even forced a slight smile. "He was bored, but otherwise fine. He complained about how much blood they keep taking from him."

Swan smiled, too. "He doesn't like having blood taken at the best of times."

With the atmosphere calmer, less combative, Swan began to relax. Her near nakedness no longer made her feel uneasy, but aroused. The gentle rubbing of her nipples on the soft, silky material. The teasing drift of the robe beneath the belt. And Travis was handsome, in a rough kind of way. She wondered why she had never thought of him like that before.

She was beginning to almost enjoy the slightly out-of-control feeling that once again invaded her mind.

"We should console each other," she said, unfastening the belt and letting the dressing gown flow freely. She felt it slide off her right nipple and move over her hip as she stepped forward. The thrill of exposing herself to her husband's best friend was almost more than she could bear. She cared about nothing but his seduction. She would not be satisfied until she felt him inside her.

"What the fuck are you doing!" Travis backed away,

pushing her as he did so. "Dennis is my best friend, and he's in hospital. What's wrong with you?"

She hesitated, shame and embarrassment fighting the thrill and excitement in her head. He was right. What was she doing? But she wanted him. And not just him, but any man. Any *woman* for that matter.

No! That's not me. Is it? What have I become? What's happening to me?

She snatched her dressing gown closed and fell back into the armchair, sobbing uncontrollably. She didn't understand what was happening. Why she was thinking these terrible, frightening thoughts.

"What's going on, Swan?" Travis's voice was a little softer now. "And don't tell me it's because of the stress of Dennis being taken into hospital. I'm pretty certain this isn't the first time you've tried something like this."

He sat on the couch opposite her and perched forward on the edge of the seat cushion.

"Are you cheating on Dennis?" He could see she was genuinely distressed, disturbed even. "Tell me, Swan. What the hell is going on?"

"I don't know what's going on," said Swan, looking up at him, her face streaked with tears. "I really don't know, and I'm scared, Travis. I think I might be losing my mind."

They were startled as the back door crashed open and a gust of wind blew through the house. And both of them felt a deep chill inside as they heard it breathe, "*Swwwaaaaannnnnnhhhiiillldddd.*"

Dennis sat on the edge of the hospital bed. He had not slept.

He had tried. Over thirty minutes of lying there, listening to someone further down the ward snoring, someone else shouting out gibberish with unforecast regularity. He had given up, preferring to sit rather than lie.

Other than stopping by to take more blood, and making a faint comment about "getting some sleep," the ward staff ignored him.

He wanted to go home.

Nighttime on the ward was not, on the face of it, much different from daytime. It was quieter, fewer people back and forth from *who knew where* to *who cares*. And they turned some of the lights off. And most of the patients were asleep. But it was the same cold walls, the same hard beds, the same hard nurses.

In his youth, a nurse was a figure of fantasy and lust. The uniform, the stockings. One long *Carry On* film in his head. But they'd changed the uniforms, and somehow they had changed the people in them, too. They were no longer a boy's frivolous wet dream. They were undoubtedly seen in a more serious, professional light. But something of the soft, caring side had been lost in the transformation. He did not feel comforted by the nurses on the ward. He felt trapped.

He wanted to go home. To Swan. He'd said as much to one of the nurses, but she said he had to wait for the doctor to do his rounds the following morning. Then, if the doctor was happy about it, he would be allowed to go home.

Allowed.

The word stuck in his head, in his throat. He did not need to be *allowed* to leave. He could go anytime he wanted to. They couldn't stop him. He knew he could discharge himself, taking full responsibility for any repercussions on his health, at any moment. And yet, he didn't. He waited, like a chicken waiting for the farmer to decide whether he got to lay another egg or ended up in the oven. He knew his rights, but he was scared to use them. The hospitals, the doctors, were in charge. They were the authorities, and all the patients, all the bed numbers on some administrator's computer screen, did as they were told.

They waited.

He waited. He was too scared to do anything else. And he hated society for making him so.

The harsh rattle of the trolley forewarned him of the arrival of a nurse with another needle.

"Time for some more blood, Mister Parkes," she said, barely raising a smile.

"I hear voices," said Dennis, unresisting as more blood was drawn. "At home. When I'm alone. I hear voices."

"Really," said the nurse, without looking up. "You should probably see someone about that."

"My friend thinks the house is haunted. I think I might be mad."

"Well, agree to disagree, that's what I always say. All done, Mister Parkes. You should lie down and get some sleep."

He watched the nurse walk away, pushing the rattling trolley ahead of her. The someone who snored still snored in another bay of the ward, even louder than the trolley. The patient who shouted had not done so for some time. At least, he presumed it was a patient. Perhaps it was one of the nurses, finally screaming out their frustration and anger.

I need to be home. I shouldn't be here. What if the voices call me and I'm not there to hear? I need to be with Swan. She is my rock, my anchor. I have to be near her to be safe.

49

Despite his fear, his lifetime of obeying convention, he stood and walked towards the nurses' station.

"We imagined it," said Swan with determination. "It's all this talk from Dennis. We're hearing words when it's really only sounds."

"It's called *audio pareidolia*," said Travis. "I experienced the same thing myself the other night, in my apartment. The same sort of thing can happen with seeing things in shadows and shapes that aren't there."

"You think that's what happened to Dennis when he was scared out of the house?"

"I'd prefer to believe that than the only other option."

"You mean that he actually saw something." Swan nodded thoughtfully. "Still doesn't mean anything was actually there. Maybe he's hallucinating? Dennis has been acting a little odd lately. It's been getting worse ever since the redundancy."

"It hit him harder than expected," said Travis. "He doesn't like to talk about it, but it knocked his self-confidence badly. But, to be fair, he's not the only one who's been acting odd."

Swan said nothing for a moment, staring at the floor. She knew what Travis was referring to, and that they hadn't finished talking about it before the wind decided to interrupt matters. But now that she was no longer crying and had calmed herself a little, she wasn't sure she wanted to continue the conversation. But, equally, she didn't think Travis would let it alone.

"I don't know what's going on with me," she said finally. "It's not exactly blackouts, but I do become only vaguely aware of what I'm doing, and have absolutely no control over it."

"Have you tried resisting?"

"When it first happens, I don't want to resist. Even though it doesn't feel like me doing it, I'm quite happy to let it happen and just watch. Only afterwards, when I'm in control again, do I feel disgusted with myself." She shook her head. "It's hard to explain properly."

"I think you should see the doctor," said Travis. "Maybe there's some medication he can put you on? And you need to talk to Dennis at some point."

"It'll destroy him."

"Better he hears it from you than me, or someone else."

Swan nodded her agreement. She knew Travis was right, but she dreaded the thought of it.

The house phone rang, startling both of them. After the second ring, Swan answered it.

Travis waited while Swan talked briefly on the phone. When she replaced the receiver, she looked concerned.

"What's wrong?"

"That was the cardiac ward," she said. "Dennis is insisting on discharging himself. They've convinced him to at least wait until someone can pick him up. He was all ready to just walk out of there."

"What are they saying about his health?"

"They got the blood work back. He didn't have a heart attack, but that means they have no idea what caused the pain."

Travis sighed, wiping a hand over tired eyes. "If he had any sense, he'd stay there and get more tests done. You don't get pains like that for nothing."

"They've tried reasoning with him, but he insists

he's coming home. There's not a lot they can do."

"Okay," said Travis. "I'll go and get him. You want to come along?"

"No." Swan looked to the floor. "I need some time before I see Dennis. I need to work out what I'm going to say, and when."

Travis pulled his car keys out of his jeans pocket, rattling them absentmindedly.

"Fair enough. Are you sure you'll be okay here on your own after... you know."

Swan forced a smile. "I'll be fine. It was just the wind, and our over-active imaginations. Despite what you tell Dennis, ghosts don't exist."

Travis laughed. "I know that. I'm only kidding with him. Ghosts are entertainment, watching people who should know better screaming and running away from the slightest noise."

"Maybe you should make that clear to Dennis? He's not as sure as you."

With a smile, Travis turned to leave, stopped and looked back. "Are you absolutely sure you don't want to come along?"

"I'm sure."

"And you're okay here on your own?"

"I'll be fine."

She watched Travis leave, not moving until she heard his car pull away from outside the house. It wouldn't take him long to get Dennis from the hospital, and she needed to compose herself, get dressed, and be ready to face him. She was so relieved he had not suffered a heart attack, but all the same, she wished he'd stayed in the hospital. Both for his own sake, and for hers.

She shivered as she stood. It seemed to have got

colder suddenly, so much so that she checked the back door wasn't still open, and that all the windows were closed. Maybe she should put the heating on before Dennis got home, warm the place up for him? The night must be getting cold quickly. She had not felt the chill while Travis was there.

Pulling her dressing gown tight about her, she went upstairs.

CHAPTER TEN

Fortunately for Travis, as he never felt comfortable in hospitals, most of the paperwork for Dennis's self-discharge had been done by the time he got to the ward. Dennis was just signing the waiver that made sure the hospital could not be blamed for anything. He looked up as Travis approached, and there were clear signs of disappointment in his eyes.

"Swan's waiting for you at home," said Travis, guessing where the disappointment lay. "She's a bit too emotional to be safe driving."

Dennis nodded, saying nothing.

Travis watched as his friend walked out of the cardiac ward ahead of him. He didn't think that Dennis had put on any actual weight, but he somehow looked heavier, or at least looked like carrying the weight was beginning to be more than he could handle. He shuffled, he slumped. Travis could hear his breathing, hard and ragged.

Dennis took the stairs down the two floors to the

ground. Travis was not surprised. Dennis didn't like lifts. Too enclosed. Too many people. He had once admitted to Travis, with the help of alcohol, that on the few occasions when he had to use a lift, he felt the other occupants were looking at him and deciding that, if anything went wrong, it would be his fault. Because of his weight.

Travis matched his pace with Dennis's as they exited the hospital. Was he walking slower than usual? Travis thought he was.

Getting in and out of cars had been something of a struggle for Dennis for some time, but as Dennis climbed into the passenger seat of Travis's car, Travis could not avoid thinking that it seemed even more of a struggle than normal.

Perhaps it was just tiredness. He doubted Dennis got much, if any, sleep in the ward that night.

"Have you noticed the people looking?" It was the first time Dennis had spoken since Travis's arrival.

"What people?" Travis started the car and eased it into the one-way lanes of the car park.

"Everyone. Looking at me. Thinking, 'Look at that fat bastard'."

"No one's looking, Dennis. You're imagining it."

"No, I'm not," said Dennis, his voice hardening angrily. "They're all thinking it. Watching me getting into the car, or just walking, or just *being*. All of them. They don't know me, but they're judging me."

Travis sighed. He had heard Dennis like this before, but usually only when they were both a little drunk. "No one is judging you," he said, keeping his voice low and even as he inserted his ticket into the machine at the car park exit, then waited for the barrier to rise.

"It's the last acceptable prejudice," said Dennis as

Travis drove away from the hospital. "It's okay to laugh at fat people, to call them names, to hate them and blame them for costing the NHS money. Anorexia is an illness, but obesity isn't. It's a condition you are solely responsible for. You're too skinny? You're ill. You're too fat? You're a lazy slob, stuffing your face with food all the time."

"You really are on one, aren't you," said Travis, shaking his head. "What's brought all this on? We were all worried you'd had a heart attack, and the way you're going now, you'll give yourself one."

"Just one less fat person draining the country's money."

"Bullshit, Dennis," said Travis, but inside he now felt guilty at the way he had been watching his friend in the hospital. The way he had been thinking about his weight and how he carried it. It made him wonder if there was some truth in what Dennis said. After all, if he, as Dennis's best friend, could wonder about his weight, who knew what others who didn't know the man might think?

Dennis paused and seemed to calm himself. When he next spoke, he sounded less angry, but still agitated. "Have you any idea how many times I was told I needed to lose weight while I was on that ward? Every doctor, most of the nurses. All said in the nicest of tones, of course, but the message was clear. Lose weight or next time it might really be a heart attack."

"I guess they're trying to be helpful."

"By telling me things I already know? Do they really think I'm that stupid? If I could click my fingers and lose weight, I'd do it. But it's not that easy."

"I know."

"There's something in my head that makes me eat

crap, even when I know I shouldn't. It's not that I don't know how to eat healthily, I just don't. I can't explain it. It's a type of mental illness, every bit as much as my depresssion or my social anxiety is. But people don't see it that way."

"I'm sure the doctors do." They were not far from Dennis's home now, and Travis had to admit he was relieved. Seeing Dennis in this mood while sober was difficult to handle. He wanted to help his friend, but he had no idea how.

"Most of my life is utter shit, Travis. Except for you and, of course, Swan. Everything else is shit."

Travis said nothing as he turned onto Wyatt Road. He felt so sorry for Dennis, knowing the bombshell that waited for him. He was certain Swan was going to come clean about what she'd been up to, and Travis did not like to think of the effect this would have on Dennis. Perhaps, even though he had suggested it, now was not the right time. He would have to stop Swan before she gave anything away. Dennis needed a chance to get out of his current dark place before he was pushed right back in it again.

He pulled the car to a stop outside number 20. The lights were on, upstairs and downstairs, but there was no sign of movement. He had thought that Swan might come to the door. Maybe she just hadn't heard them arrive.

He waited while Dennis climbed out, and then the two of them walked down the driveway, past Swan's pink Corsa and Dennis's Peugeot. Dennis used his own key to unlock the front door, and they went inside. There was still no sign of Swan.

"Swan?" called Travis as they entered. "He's home."

There was no answer. He watched Dennis drop

into his favourite armchair. He looked tired, completely drained, both physically and mentally.

"I'll just pop upstairs and see what's keeping her," said Travis.

Not waiting for any kind of reply, he hurried up the stairs. "Swan?"

He stopped on the landing, suddenly anxious. The door to the bedroom was slightly ajar, and items of clothing, mostly Swan's underwear, were strewn around the entrance. Cautiously, he pushed the door fully open. Inside, the bedroom was a complete mess, drawers open, clothes thrown everywhere, makeup, books, magazines, everything scattered about. The windows were open and, for a moment, Travis remembered the sudden wind that had startled them both earlier. Had it really been safe to leave Swan alone?

As he stepped through the door, an icy cold scratched at his skin, much colder than could be explained by the open windows. He peeked nervously around the bed, half expecting to find a body on the floor. Swan was not there.

She wasn't in the house. He could feel it. Had she run away rather than face Dennis? Even though he had considered it earlier, he didn't believe she would do that. Neither did he believe she would leave the room in such a mess voluntarily, with her clothes and magazines strewn about the place. It did not fit the Swan he knew.

But if she hadn't left, where was she? And if she'd been taken by force, why and by whom?

He had left her alone. He had said ghosts didn't exist. Had he been wrong? But ghosts didn't make people disappear, did they?

Perhaps she *had* just left? Run away rather than admit to Dennis what she'd been up to. As much as he doubted it, nothing else made sense.

But worse than any of that, how did he tell Dennis?

PART II
BRI✝✝A

CHAPTER ELEVEN

Professor Simon Forrester parked his Land Rover on the main road into Anbal. There was no sign telling him this was Ottmor Wood, but it was the first significant grouping of trees he'd seen since his Sat Nav insisted he had *arrived at his destination*. He climbed out and stretched his back. The drive from the university had only taken a little over thirty minutes, yet he felt like he'd been sitting in the driver's seat for hours.

"You must be getting old, Professor." Britta Lange, a third-year Archaeology student, stepped out the passenger side of the Land Rover. She reached up behind her head to tie back shoulder-length blonde hair and unconsciously pushed her breasts forward, stretching the Blink-182 t-shirt she wore.

Simon, aware that he was staring more than he should, reminded himself that she was his student, and looked away. He had already lost his wife and, five years ago, almost his job. Since then he had resisted temptation successfully. He was determined not make the same mistakes again.

It was with some relief that he saw his other third-year student, Scott Bays, unpacking the bags from the back of the car. Although Scott didn't know it, he was along as a *chaperon*, to make sure Simon behaved himself.

"Jake and Elton said they'd meet us here," said Simon, concentrating on the reason they had driven down from Taupington. His obsession with his work was the one thing stronger than the allure of female students. "I don't think we're too early."

"Right on time, Professor," said Jake as he and Elton stepped out of the shadows of the wood and leaned on the wooden fence that marked the boundary of Ottmor Wood on the main road side.

Although Simon had never seen pictures of Jake and Elton, he had corresponded with them regularly on email since that first contact six months ago. They looked very much as he had imagined them. Both wore old jeans, classic rock t-shirts under open hoodies (one was AC/DC, the other Led Zeppelin), and had unruly hair, almost as long as Britta's, although both were muddy brown in colour. One of them wore a woollen hat.

"Jake and Elton I presume?" he said, stepping forward to shake hands.

"I'm Jake," said the hatless one, taking the offered hand. "This is Elton."

"Nice to finally meet you." Simon stepped back, having shaken hands with both.

"It's been six months, Professor," said Elton. "Long time."

"I'm sorry about that. The university works very slowly, and I had to get their permission and agreement

on some basic funding. Plus, I had to organise my team."
He pointed to the two students, standing, smiling, just
behind him. "This is Britta and Scott."

Nods and hellos were offered all round, with some
awkwardness, particularly from Elton, and then Jake
and Elton led the way into Ottmor Wood.

The team from the university was well prepared.
Their boots had no difficulty with the sometimes soft,
muddy ground underfoot. Jake and Elton, however, did
their best to avoid those areas, as they always did. Their
sneakers were not quite so robust.

"I noticed the sign for one of the places we passed
through just up the road. It had the old Viking name
underneath," said Simon as they walked.

"You mean Thingwall," said Jake.

"Yes, that was the one. *Ping-vollr*. Assembly field."

"There's even a Viking re-enactment group around,"
said Elton, unable to suppress a snorting laugh.

"They call themselves Wirhalh Skip Felagr," said
Jake.

Elton almost stumbled as he turned his head to stare
incredulously at his friend. "How the fuck do you know
that?"

Jake shrugged. "My dad's a member."

It looked as though Elton was about to respond,
in less than complimentary terms, when Britta cut in.
"The Professor thinks this stone you found is connected to Vikings, too."

"Yes," said Simon. "The few letters I've been able
to make out so far suggest an Old Norse word."

They had reached the clearing, and Jake and Elton
perched themselves on their fallen tree trunk.

"Well, here we are," said Jake. "We've been doing
our best to keep it cleaned off until you could get

here."

"You've done a great job," said Simon, looking at the near-perfect rectangular sandstone block at the edge of the clearing. "It's magnificent."

He knelt alongside it, running his fingers over the carved lettering. "Just as I thought," he said quietly to himself, before turning to his two students. "Get everything set up so we can document, measure, examine, all the usual things. And search the surrounding area for anything else that might be lying around."

"Can we dig?" said Scott, unpacking pointing trowels and brushes from his backpack.

"I'll need to get permission first. But I think we have more than enough evidence here for the university to get it sorted."

"I don't mean to interrupt," said Jake. "Now that you're all getting started and everything. But maybe you could tell us what the thing actually says? I mean, once you've examined it properly. It's been driving us nuts trying to work it out."

"I can tell you that right now," said Simon, grinning. "I already had my suspicions before we got here, but being able to trace the last few letters confirms it. It says *Gjallarbru*."

"Which means?" said Elton.

"In Norse mythology, *Gjallarbru* is the bridge that connects the worlds of the living and the dead."

CHAPTER TWELVE

Swan's car still stood in the driveway, its pink body-work a lonely beacon as Travis turned onto Wyatt Road. It blocked Dennis's Peugeot, but that didn't matter. Dennis hadn't left the house in almost six months.

The signs of neglect were obvious, as Travis pulled to the kerb. Weeds, a constant annoyance and regular maintenance job for Swan, now flourished along the edge of the driveway. The windows of the house were streaked and dirty, the window cleaners giving up after two months of no communication and no payment from Dennis.

Travis edged past the cars to the front door, feeling a little guilty. It had been almost a week since he had last visited. Work had been hectic. It was a long time to leave Dennis on his own, and he was worried. It made him hesitate before he entered the house, using a spare key Spencer had given him.

The smell inside the house was of unbinned garbage, wrestling with the musty smell of unwashed clothes and uncleaned carpets. Every flat surface he looked at as he entered the hallway was thick with dust. The little, unnoticed things that Swan would do around the house, and Dennis, too, at times, were no longer done. If he had not known otherwise, he would have thought the house deserted.

"Dennis, it's just me," he called as he closed the front door behind him. "Sorry I've not been round."

He found Dennis where he expected him to be, in the front room, slumped in his armchair, staring blankly ahead at the TV. There was a vague nod of the head in acknowledgement of Travis's arrival.

"Have you been remembering your pills?" Sorting Dennis's medication was one of the tasks Travis would do when he visited. But in-between times, Dennis had to get his own.

"Couldn't be bothered," said Dennis, his voice low, almost inaudible.

Travis sighed. He had suspected as much. "You know it makes you worse if you don't take them."

"What could be worse than Swan leaving me?"

Travis said nothing. There was no way he could answer that often-asked question without making it worse. Instead, he chose to redirect. "What are you watching?"

The TV was turned low, barely audible, and the screen showed something that looked suspiciously like one of the Australian soaps.

"No idea."

"Then why have it on?"

"Better than silence."

Travis cleared the plates, dishes, and cups from around Dennis's chair. Without speaking, he took them into the kitchen and put them on one of the cluttered work units. He needed to sort Dennis's pills out, get the dishwasher and the washer going. Most of all, he needed to avoid the possibility of his frustration bursting over into anger

He wanted to yell at Dennis that it had been six months, and he should be at least *starting* to pull himself together. He wanted to tell him that he still had a life without Swan. He wanted to tell him that he wasn't even sure that Swan had left, at least not in the way that Dennis believed. But which would be worse for Dennis? Thinking his wife left him, or that she was forcefully taken by someone, or some *thing*?

Swan just up and leaving was difficult for Travis to accept. Despite her increasingly strange behaviour leading up to the disappearance, she still seemed to love her husband. When he had gone to get Dennis from the hospital, she had been worried, thoughtful even, but seemed ready to talk. The state of her bedroom, the underwear thrown about, just didn't add up to Swan leaving voluntarily. And then there was her car. She loved her car, and yet it remained parked in the driveway.

The police had not been impressed with his reasoning. They saw no signs of a struggle, no evidence of blood or other bodily fluids. Swan was an adult, and it was not their business to get involved in a domestic situation. If she wanted to leave, she was within her rights to do so. They did not consider there was any case worth investigating.

Travis felt instinctively that they were wrong, but he could think of no way to prove it. All he could do was visit the house two or three times a week and make sure Dennis took his pills and had something to eat and drink. He kept promising himself he would clean, tidy the mess up a little. But he felt so consistently demoralised on each visit that he could never bring himself to start on what would, undoubtedly, be a long, arduous task.

Dennis had plummeted to a depth of depression Travis had never witnessed before, but he refused to see or talk to anyone other than Travis. Even a home visit by Dr. Banks had been turned away. All Travis could do was the basics needed to keep Dennis alive. He had no idea how to help his friend even *begin* to escape from the clutches of the illness that was destroying his life.

Travis had left some hours ago. Dennis was certain of that. He was alone again, and that's how he preferred it.

He had always known Swan could do better than him. While he had a good job and kept reasonably fit, he just about managed to hold on to her. But, ever since the redundancy and the rapid weight gain, he had been waiting for the day she left.

Even so, when it actually happened, it was a gut-tearing wrench. A killing strike at his whole life. What *was* his life without Swan anyway? Nothing. Empty. If he'd had the courage to carry it through, he would have killed himself. He had considered it, planned the ways he could do it, even held a blade to his wrist, poured out an overdose of his pills. But in the end, he could not take those final steps. He could not face the pain or the sickness that would precede death. And, even worse, what if he failed? While he would happily let someone else do the deed for him, he could not push himself to suicide. He was a failure in that, as well as everything else.

Swan was not to be blamed. She stuck with him longer than he had expected. But, eventually, she had to leave for her own sanity. Living with him must have been driving her crazy. He hoped she was safe and happy somewhere, things she could not be with him.

At some point, he might switch the TV off and go to bed. Or he might just sleep in the chair, as he did quite often these days. Why struggle upstairs to bed when Swan was not there to share it with him?

He was almost dozing off when the susurration began, the sibilant whispering.

He had not heard voices in the house, nor seen darting shadows or strange figures, since Swan left. For them to start again for no apparent reason startled him awake.

The main feeling was one of disappointment, even annoyance. He thought he was rid of them. Unlike Swan, he was happy *they* had gone. Now, they were back.

The whispering rose in volume. Just one voice, striving to be heard. Nothing intelligible, not at first. Then, through a hissing, crackling static, he heard one word that sent a chill through his bones.

"*Dennis.*"

But it wasn't the word that chilled him the most. It was the voice.

It was Swan!

CHAPTER THIRTEEN

Alison Hoggarth checked the clock on the apartment wall. Just after 7:00 pm. She kicked her shoes off, hung her coat on the row of hooks behind the door, and walked gingerly into her bedroom. With the door shut, she peeled off her work clothes and her underwear, glad of the release.

Standing naked in front of the mirror, she did not like what she saw. She was possibly a little overweight, but only in as much as there was a roundness to her tummy and a firmness to her thighs. Nothing that anyone else would find abhorrent. Her hair was brown and long, almost reaching her elbows. She did not consider herself pretty, but she certainly didn't think she was ugly. In fact, there was nothing at all wrong with the way she looked, and yet she didn't like it. And there was always one negative she could focus on, always there, always reliable. She looked tired, with heavy bags under her eyes. She *was* tired!

She worked long hours in the offices of a local firm, Leonard & Ford Accountants. Other than Mr. Leonard and Mr. Ford themselves, there were only two of them working in the office: Alison, and Jean Ford, Mr. Ford's daughter. Between them, they did everything from filing, letters, photocopying, dealing with any members of the public who might phone or drop in, to being Personal Assistants to the two owners. Some nights, as she rested her aching feet, stretched her aching back, and massaged the pain in her left wrist that she worried might develop into carpel tunnel syndrome, she wondered why she worked there.

The pay was above minimum wage, but not by much. The hours were long, and the work constant and punishing. It was true that the commute was short, being a local firm based in the main street of Anbal, but that in itself was not enough to keep her there. Jean's reason for working in the office was obvious, being the family firm. But why didn't Alison look for better paid, less arduous work elsewhere?

She knew the answer, but was embarrassed to admit it, even to herself. It was Mr. Leonard. She adored Mr. Leonard, perhaps even loved him. She wasn't sure. She'd never loved anyone before, not like this. She would lie in bed some nights, whispering his first name to her pillow, "*Edgar*," as though he were there alongside her. But he never would be. He was married to a beautiful woman and had two adorable children. They had money; they seemed happy. She could not compete with that. She had nothing to offer, so she worshipped from afar and stayed in a dead-end job, with low pay and long hours, just so she could be close to him.

"You're pathetic," she said, quietly to her reflection in the bedroom mirror. "Thirty-one years old and going soft over a married man at least twenty years older. How low can you get?"

She fell silent as she heard her brother and Jake turning the key in the apartment door, talking about some rubbish she had no interest in. She smiled at her reflection.

"Well, there is always *someone* lower."

She laughed, stopping abruptly as she heard her brother call from the other room.

"Is that you, sis?"

"Of course," she said, almost laughing again while she checked the bolt on her bedroom door was slid across. Maybe it was hysteria?

"It's just us."

That was Jake. He seemed a little smarter than Elton, but not by much.

What were her parents thinking, giving her brother a name like Elton? It was obvious they named him after Elton John, who they still played *ad nauseam* on their CD system at home. Then again, she suspected *she* was named after a song by Elvis Costello. But at least that was a little more subtle.

She turned to the old oak chest of drawers adjacent to the mirror and began to dress, chuckling to herself as she thought of her flatmates.

Jake and Elton. Anbal's answer to Jay and Silent Bob. But not as funny.

"So, what have you two been doing while the rest of us work our asses off?" Alison stepped out of her bedroom in loose t-shirt and jeans. When at home, comfort was the word.

"Remember that stone we uncovered in Ottmor Wood?" said Jake, trying not to notice the obviously bra-less breasts that moved in disconcerting ways under her t-shirt as Alison walked to the kitchen. He had grown up with Elton, and Elton's sister should be just that. His best friend's sister, nothing else. A sexless, uninteresting irritant who had been there all of his life. It seemed wrong to see her as a woman, and an attractive one at that.

"The one you emailed the university about?" Alison made herself a coffee, not bothering to offer one to either of her flatmates, as they both had Pepsi Max cans in their hands.

"They finally turned up," said Jake.

"And Jake thinks one of the students is hot." Elton smiled wickedly, enjoying the look of embarrassment on his friend's face.

"No," said Jake quickly. "She's just nice, that's all. I never said *hot*."

"And what about you, Elton?" Alison sat in the armchair across from the settee where Elton and Jake sprawled. "Do *you* think she's hot?"

Elton's smile faded as he shook his head. "She's not my type."

"We have yet to find what Elton's type is," said Jake, savouring the chance to get back at his friend. "But no doubt this perfect woman will eventually turn up. He's just keeping himself for her, aren't you, Elton."

"Something like that." The words were almost mumbled as Elton lifted his soda can and emptied the last drops.

"Anyway," said Alison, steering the conversation away from the usual insults flung back and forth by the two friends. "Apart from one of them being *nice*, what else is going on?"

"The Professor was really interested," said Jake. "He said he's going to try and convince the university to fund a proper dig there. But, for the moment, it's just the three of them."

"They were still there when we left," said Elton, speaking clearly once more. "Wouldn't fancy working in there at night."

"Presumably they have somewhere booked to stay?" said Alison.

"No idea." Jake shook his soda can and was disappointed to find it empty. "Never asked them. But I'm sure they have."

CHAP+ER FØUR+EEN

Scott Bays knew he had no chance with Britta Lange. It was not something that bothered him much, despite the constant comments from his friends. To them, it was impossible to work alongside a beautiful girl without trying to hit on her. He did not deny that Britta was beautiful, but above all else, she was a fellow archaeology student, and currently his colleague on Professor Forrester's latest expedition. And if he *had* tried to hit on her, he knew she was out of his league. He wasn't stupid. However, he did sometimes wonder whether Forrester was.

"What do you think about this stone?" He sipped coffee in the back of the Land Rover, Britta seated alongside him.

"Could be interesting," said Britta, preferring tea to coffee. "But could equally just be a stone somebody scratched an old word on. I'm not sure how much significance can be placed on it."

"Forrester seems convinced it's important. He's already phoned Vance three times, pushing for a full-fledged dig here."

Professor Fritz Vance, Forrester's boss at the university, had not sounded happy at being, in the word they had heard snapped over the phone, *hounded*.

"I mean, I think it's a bit creepy," said Britta. "You know, this stone in the ground with *Gjallarbru* scratched on it. But I'd be even more creeped out if it was in the middle of a river somewhere."

"This wood doesn't exactly look like the river *Gioll* does it?"

"Of course, we could be taking all this mythology a little too literally," said Britta, and the two students began to laugh. It was an in-joke among the students that one of Professor Forrester's pet hates was people who looked at mythology from a literal point of view, insisting that what was written was either solid fact or complete fantasy. While the students agreed with Forrester's view of mythology as storytelling conveying a basic, underlying truth, they nevertheless found it amusing to every now and then press Forrester's buttons and bring up a literal interpretation of whatever mythology was the subject of the latest archaeological find.

"I dare you to ask him if he thinks there's an underground river around here," said Scott, smiling.

"There *is* a little brook further along," said Britta. "Maybe that's it? Just as little smaller than the myth claims."

They fell silent as Professor Forrester pulled open the front passenger door of the Land Rover and leaned inside.

"You two finished your drinks yet?" said the Professor, curls of hair flattened to his head with sweat. "I could do with some help."

The students finished their drinks quickly, Scott hoping the Professor had not heard what they had been saying. It was with some guilt that he returned the cup to the top of the thermos, looking across at Britta as she did the same with her own. If she felt guilty, she didn't show it. He felt sure it was written all over his face.

They followed Simon Forrester back into Ottmor Wood, stepping carefully in the rapidly fading light.

Britta stayed close behind Professor Forrester, knowing that Scott was equally close behind her. She liked Scott and was glad he had been chosen to come along on this trip. Scott was nice. She felt comfortable and safe with him.

She was less sure about Professor Forrester. There were rumours about him, and he did come across as a bit of a *lech* sometimes. But he had never tried anything with her, and he was a very good teacher. That alone superseded unfounded gossip in her mind. She wanted to be an archaeologist, ever since she could remember. She might joke with Scott about it, but she hoped Forrester was right and this stone was important. To be involved in an important dig right from the very start would make her final year spectacular. And it couldn't hurt when it came to the final degree. And then her Masters. It was not unheard of, in the field, for one important dig to make an archaeologist's name. It could even form the basis for her Ph.D.! She was nothing if not ambitious.

"I've been trying to see if the thing could be lifted, if we get the funding to do this site properly," said Forrester as he stopped in the clearing. "At the moment I can't budge it an inch."

"You want to see if we can manage it all together?" said Britta as she and Scott joined the Professor alongside the stone.

"That's the idea," said Forrester. "But just before we get started, I'd like to get a couple of things straight." The Professor turned to his two students, his face stern. "First of all, Britta, *Gjallarbru* is not *scratched* on this stone, it is *carved*, and with a lot of care."

Britta flushed and lowered her eyes. Her stomach turned. This was so embarrassing, like being caught out at school. He must have heard some of what they were saying before he opened the car door.

"And to both of you, *no*," continued Forrester. "I am not expecting to find some underground river here. You *are* taking the mythology too literally, and you know exactly how I feel about that!"

Britta glanced over at Scott and saw him looking every bit as uneasy as she felt. Forrester hadn't just heard *some* of what they said; he must have been standing out there listening the whole time. She felt both guilty and a little creeped out thinking of him standing there, just listening.

"Now," said Forrester. "With that out of the way, help me move this thing. Just enough to know it could be done with the proper tools." He smiled, and Britta felt the tension ease. "Then we'll go to the hotel and get settled in for the night."

Simon Forrester did not enjoy *pulling rank* on his students, but he had expected more from Britta and

Scott. When he had gone to the car for their help and heard them talking, he decided to listen a moment, curious as to what they might be saying. With a view through the window, knowing that with the light inside they would be unlikely to notice him in the gathering dusk, he had watched Britta. Her hair, the way her mouth moved when she spoke, the way her t-shirt swelled with her breasts and then fell to her lap. And her legs. He had stopped to look as much as to listen, and had hoped to catch some gossip about other students, or Britta's love life.

Instead, what he heard made the anger boil inside him. He had personally chosen these two for this trip, and he did not expect to hear them spouting nonsense about actual rivers beneath an actual bridge acting as a boundary between the living and the dead. Even if they were joking, it was not what he wanted to hear from them.

With that out of the way, there were more important things on his mind.

"Let's give this a try," he said, waving to Scott to get the other side of the stone, and Britta to squat alongside him. "Now remember, straight backs and push up with your legs. I don't want either of you pulling anything. We're not trying to lift it completely clear, just move it a little."

They all took hold as best they could, digging fingers down at the side of the stone to get a grip underneath. Simon had dug out a little around the stone while Britta and Scott were on their coffee break, and they could see the stone went deeper than they first thought. Even so, they wanted to see if it was loosened at all.

"1... 2... 3!"

On Simon's count, they all took the strain, trying

to lift the stone. It wouldn't move. They tried again and again, but without success.

"It almost feels like something's holding it back," said Scott. "Not just the weight of the thing, but something actually holding on to it under there."

"Can you two keep hold just in case the thing suddenly drops?" said Simon. "I'm going to dig a little more down there and see if you're right."

While Britta and Scott kept their hands on the stone, just as a precaution, Simon grabbed a trowel and stretched himself out on the muddy ground. He reached deep into the hole he had dug around the stone earlier and stabbed at what seemed to be the base of the stone. The ground was tough, and several times his wrist jarred as the trowel blade hit solid rock rather than softer earth. But he kept poking and scraping away.

"Fuck me, I think you're right!" It wasn't often he swore in front of his students, but he felt this merited it. "Make sure you've got hold of that thing."

He shuffled forwards, leaning further into the hole, peering into the small gap he had made with the trowel. The side of his face was pressed into the mud, but he didn't care. There actually was something under the rock. It didn't look like sandstone, didn't look like rock at all. It was thick, knotted, and marked with the grain of wood. Yet it seemed to grow out of the rock, or the rock grew out of it. There was no visible way such a thing could be attached to a block of sandstone, not enough to hold it in place with them tugging at the rock. And yet he could not deny the evidence of his eyes.

With a glance up at his students to confirm they still had hold of the rock, he reached into the small gap, stretching his fingers as far as he could. Touching it, he knew at once that it was, indeed, wood, or at the very least, vegetable in origin. Certainly not stone.

"It's like some huge root," he said, almost to himself. "The root of the stone. But that's ridiculous."

He managed to reach up to where vegetable met mineral, but there was no joint he could feel. Nothing to indicate that these were two different things linked together. They simply merged. He knew that was impossible. It could only be that he just couldn't feel where they joined. Once it was lifted free by the proper equipment, he would be able to study it properly.

He touched the *root* once more, pushing his fingers harder against it. And that was when he felt it. Slow and regular.

The *root* had a pulse.

CHAP+ER FIF+EEN

The call from Dennis had taken Travis completely by surprise. His friend sounded so animated on the phone, so unlike the unresponsive person he had become since Swan's disappearance that Travis actually wondered whether Dennis had taken an overdose of his pills, and this sudden animation was the precursor of a heart attack. It was with some panic that Travis agreed he would call round immediately.

Stepping out of his car, the first thing he noticed was that Dennis's front door was open. The second, as he edged past the parked cars in the driveway, was a number of black bin sacks lined up on the pathway in front of the bay window. He counted five, and as he stood there, Dennis appeared in the doorway and threw another onto the pile.

"Travis," said Dennis, smiling. "Come in. I've got news."

Worried, Travis followed Dennis into the house,

closing the front door behind him. The musty smell was still there, along with the stench of decaying rubbish, but there were other things, too. A hint of polish. The sharp edge of bleach. Much of the dust had been cleared off surfaces, and the old Dyson stood in the centre of the front room, still plugged in to the wall socket.

"You've been cleaning," he said, stating an obvious fact, but unable to stop himself.

"I have to," said Dennis, sweat glistening on his face, showing in patches through his t-shirt. "I have to get it ready."

"For God's sake, Dennis, sit down before you collapse."

Dennis had the pale pallor of a man on the edge of fainting, or on the verge of having a heart attack or stroke. Travis tried to keep the alarm out of his voice as he sat on the settee opposite Dennis's favourite armchair.

With a look of reluctance and impatience, Dennis sat, but he sat forward, on the edge, refusing to relax.

"What's going on?" said Travis. "Have you taken anything you shouldn't have?"

"No, nothing." Dennis looked puzzled by the question. "Why?"

"You look like you're hyped up on stimulants. What's going on?"

"I promise you, I've taken nothing. I just have to get the house ready."

"Ready for what?" Travis shook his head. "You're not making sense, and you're going to kill yourself if you carry on like this."

"But..."

"You're not fit enough to run around," interrupted Travis. "If you push yourself too far... well, at the very least you'll suffer for it tomorrow, with your back and your joints."

"I'm sorry," said Dennis, stiffly trying to relax back into the armchair. "I guess I've just been excited. I have a reason to live again. I have something to look forward to."

"What's happened? Tell me, Dennis. I'm not complaining, but I'd like to know what's given you this new lease of life." Travis smiled grimly. "Last time I saw you, you were on the verge of disappearing altogether, you'd become so withdrawn. Now you're more *out there* than I've seen you in twenty years or more. Just tell me what the fuck is going on?"

"Sorry, I'm not thinking straight. Too much to do." Dennis sat forward again, smiling. "She's coming home. I know it. Swan is coming home."

"Have you heard from her?" Travis was wary. This news didn't fit with his assessment of the disappearance. He really didn't think Swan was in any position to just *come home*. Of course, he could be wrong. "What makes you so sure?"

"The whispering is back."

Travis felt his stomach turn, his heart accelerate. The one good thing about Swan's going was that the whispering and the manifestations had stopped. He believed the shock had finally snapped Dennis's brain out of whatever was causing the delusions. Now, it seemed, it was starting again. But it still didn't answer the question.

"Doesn't explain why you think Swan is coming back," he said, trying to keep his voice steady.

"But she's in the whispers, Travis," said Dennis. "I can hear her, calling me. She wants to come home. She's on her way. I know it."

Travis wasn't sure what the expression on Dennis's

face was, but it looked to border on the manic, an almost religious fervour and belief. It scared him.

"I think we should get you to Doctor Banks," said Travis, keeping his voice low and calm. "You should have a chat with him. I'll make an appointment first thing in the morning."

Dennis shook his head, almost laughing.

"I'm not crazy. Really, I'm not." He glanced towards the wall clock. "If you wait a few minutes, I can prove it to you. Since they started up again, the whispers have been quite regular."

Travis said nothing as Dennis once more relaxed back into the chair, a little less stiffly this time. He wasn't sure what to do. Getting Dennis to the doctor was an obvious one, but could he afford to wait until a surgery appointment in the morning? Should he call an ambulance? Was Dennis a danger to himself? He didn't like the thought of trying to forcefully manhandle Dennis out of the house to the car. Dennis was big, heavy, and strong. He had always been stronger than Travis, and it was unlikely the weight gain and loss of general health would have completely atrophied his muscles. The police? Just how crazy was Dennis?

He thought he heard a hiss, like escaping gas, and looked around the room for the source. The hiss grew, as did his unease. It became more than one hiss, multiple sounds, building to a static-like interference in his head. The sibilance of distant voices wormed through his mind, one voice growing stronger, clearer. He could hear it. Not just Dennis this time, but he was hearing it himself. He could no longer doubt his friend unless he was also going crazy.

Dennis sat opposite, grinning, happy at sharing his good news.

One word, repeated over and over, pushed out of the static, the incoherent sibilance. "*Dennis.*" And just like his friend, Travis recognised the voice, beyond any doubt.

Swan.

CHAPTER SIXTEEN

The Travelodge on the edge of Anbal was cheap enough that the university had agreed to Professor Forrester and his two students staying over rather than commuting back and forth. Even though it was only a thirty minute drive to the university, Simon Forrester wanted that time to be spent working, not driving.

He sat on the edge of the bed in the twin room he and Scott were sharing. Britta had a room of her own, just a few doors down the corridor. While Scott filled the small kettle from the bathroom sink and set it to boil, Simon thought about the *root*, and of the pulse he had felt. As though it were alive.

He had felt something else when that pulse thudded through his fingers. He had felt a certainty, a belief in the underlying truth of the Norse mythology. Not the academic belief he had always had, but a complete, all-consuming belief and understanding. The mythology told a truth. *His* truth. He was now a part of it as it began to be written again, continued into the modern age. He was instrumental in the new legends that would be enacted as others wrote them down. He had a destiny to fulfill...

"Tea or coffee?"

"What?" Simon blinked, feeling disoriented and slightly dizzy. Only gradually did he remember where he was, *who* he was.

"I was asking whether you wanted tea or coffee," said Scott. "Sorry if I startled you."

"I was just thinking," said Simon, unsure now what it was he had been thinking about. Something to do with the *root*.

"So, is it tea or coffee?"

"Tea, please," he said, watching with disinterest as Scott busied himself at the small refreshments tray. He did not understand quite what had happened to him, where his thoughts had led. But somehow he felt that it had been right. That it had been, ultimately, *him*. He could barely wait to get back to the stone, and the strange *root* beneath. The answers were there, almost within reach. He would not wait for the university to make its mind up.

CHAPTER SEVENTEEN

"It was Swan."

"It certainly sounded like her voice, a little…"

"It was Swan!"

Dennis's snapping, aggressive tone left no room for negotiation. He was convinced he had heard Swan calling his name, and no one, not even his best friend, could persuade him otherwise.

Travis realised the futility of further disagreement. Had not his underlying caution and scepticism been so strong, he would have been as certain as Dennis. He did not doubt he heard something, nor did he doubt that it sounded like a voice saying Dennis's name. And the voice had sounded like Swan. A little.

A lot, if I'm honest.

But how could it be? At best, she had left. At worst, she had been taken. She might even be dead. Whichever way it was looked at, she was not here in the house with him and Dennis. And she certainly wasn't floating around, whispering Dennis's name from out of nothing.

Unless she is *dead and has returned as a ghost.*

Travis pinched the bridge of his nose between thumb and forefinger as a headache began to pound inside his skull. Although his scepticism had been seriously knocked in the immediate aftermath of Swan's disappearance, it still outweighed the stuttering, uncertain belief that had crept in at that time. He would no longer say, outright, that he did not believe in ghosts, but he would say he seriously doubted their existence. It left the way open, just, for strong evidence to convince him otherwise.

"She's coming back to me," said Dennis, interrupting Travis's thoughts.

He looked up to see Dennis sitting on the edge of the armchair, his right leg jiggling, his foot tapping a fast but faltering rhythm on the carpeted floor. He was wringing his hands, and his smile had the stiff look of the manic.

He's about to crack. But I don't know how to save him!

"How can you be so sure she's coming back?" he said, hoping that making Dennis talk it through might calm him a little. "I'll accept that we heard her calling your name, but how do you know what that actually means?"

"What else could it mean?" said Dennis, his voice a little shaky. "She's calling me. Telling me she's on her way."

"Where from? This wasn't a phone call or an email. This was her disembodied voice coming out of thin air. Where do you think she is?"

The smile slipped a little from Dennis's face, and he looked uncertain. Travis had no wish to cause his friend distress, but at least it was making him think.

"I... I don't know," said Dennis finally. "I don't know where she is, but I know she's coming home."

Travis breathed a little easier. Dennis's body language suggested he had calmed down. The leg still trembled, but the foot no longer tapped. He still wrung his hands, but only occasionally, not constantly. Even his facial expression was a little closer to the friend Travis had known for so long.

"Being brutally honest..." said Travis.

"As you must."

Travis smiled. Dennis's response had seemed automatic, a reflex honed over many years of friendship. It showed he was almost back to his usual self.

"As I was saying," said Travis. "Being brutally honest, we don't know why we're hearing her voice. I don't know why I'm hearing *any* voices! But that aside, there's not really any indication of her purpose."

"But why else would she be calling my name?"

Travis saw a look of panic in Dennis's eyes, and he wondered if he was pushing at his beliefs too hard. Dennis had convinced himself that Swan was coming home, and the drop from that was steep and long. He still wanted to make his friend think clearly about what was happening, but he needed to be cautious in how he did it.

"Perhaps you're right," he said, keeping his voice calm and steady. "She could be coming home. I'm not ruling that out. I'm just saying we didn't hear anything that directly said that, unless you've heard more before you called me?"

Dennis said nothing, just shook his head and dropped his gaze to stare at the floor.

"Perhaps she wants to talk? Explain why she left

you," said Travis, knowing he took some risk in directly bringing up her leaving.

Dennis looked up before he spoke. His eyes glistened in the light. Tears ran down his cheeks. "Maybe she needs my help?" he said quietly. "Maybe somebody *did* take her, and she's trapped and needs my help to escape."

The possibility had crossed Travis's mind, but he had been reluctant to suggest it. He was uncertain whether to be relieved that Dennis had brought it up, or to fear how it might make Dennis act. If he thought she was trapped, he would want to rescue her somehow.

And none of this explained how she was speaking out of thin air, nor why she just spoke Dennis's name and didn't explain anything further.

"I'm going to need your help," said Dennis, looking at Travis with a disturbing directness.

"What for?"

"To work out how to rescue Swan. You have to help me."

Travis hesitated. What should he do? Dennis seemed to have replaced the conviction that Swan was coming home with one that she was trapped and needed help to escape. But where from? And where would they even start?

I can't let Dennis go through this on his own. What other choice is there?

"Of course I'll help," he said, smiling. "Just give me a little time to do some research, ask around. We need to find a starting point with all this."

Dennis nodded. "We can only rescue her once we know where she needs to be rescued *from!*"

Travis sighed quietly in relief. At least he had bought

time to try and work something out. At the moment, he could think of nothing.

CHAP+ER EIGH+EEN

Jake and Elton sauntered into Ottmor Wood from the main road to Anbal at eight the next morning. Neither had been out of the apartment this early for some time, but they were eager to arrive early and catch up with the investigation of the stone. The archaeological team was already there, scraping around the edges of the stone with their trowels.

Elton watched Jake's eyes settle on the kneeling Britta and laughed. "You've got it bad," he said. "It's almost pathetic."

Jake jabbed Elton lightly with his elbow. "Fuck you. I'm just looking. There's something wrong with you if you don't want to look at a girl like that."

Elton shrugged. "Not my type."

"They never are," said Jake, smiling. "You have to be the fussiest bastard around when it comes to women."

"I'm choosy. At least I'm not a slave to my dick like some people I know."

Jake was prevented from replying, as Scott climbed to his feet, turned, and saw them.

"Jake," he said. "Elton. Morning. Can I get you a tea or coffee? I'm just taking a short break."

"No thanks," said Jake. "I'm fine." At his side, Elton shook his head, also declining a drink. "We thought we'd come along and see how you guys are getting on."

"It's going great," said Scott, idly scraping chunks of mud and soil from the blade of his trowel. "We had an early start this morning. Simon, Professor Forrester, woke us up at five. We've been here since before six."

Elton raised his eyebrows in surprise. "That's early," he said. "I don't think I've seen five in the morning since... well, not sure I've ever seen it, to be honest."

Scott laughed. "You get used to it on these expeditions." He made a move to go past them. "I've just got to get a coffee from the car. Can't take too long a break. Not fair to the others."

"No problem," said Jake, moving slightly to let him past.

They watched Scott hurry towards the Land Rover.

"Seems a nice guy," said Elton.

Jake shrugged. "I guess. Let's see what the others are up to."

Simon had looked up from the dig when he heard Scott talking. He didn't mind Jake and Elton coming along, since they had been the ones to inform him of this find, just as long as they didn't disrupt the team. The one thing he was cautious about was how much information to give away. To his knowledge, the strange root-like fixture beneath the stone was unique. He did not want news of it leaking out to the press—or other archaeologists. He trusted Britta and Scott. They had been out with him enough times to know how it worked. Any questions about the find would be redirected to him. That was how he liked it.

"Good morning," he called without pausing in his scraping around the stone. "You decided to see what was happening?"

"Just curious," said Jake. "Find anything interesting?"

"We're just clearing around the stone at the moment. Then we'll start digging down and see what's underneath."

"Can we help at all?" Jake glanced at Elton, who nodded almost imperceptibly. "It's not like we've got anything else on today. Or most days, to be honest."

"Thanks for the offer," said Simon. "We don't need any help at the moment, but if we decide to try and move this stone, then we could use some extra muscle."

"Cool," said Jake. "Just let us know when."

Jake turned his gaze towards Britta, still kneeling, bent slightly forward, the back of her t-shirt riding up to reveal a line of pale flesh above the belt of her jeans. He felt stirrings in his stomach and his groin, and prayed to God that he didn't get a hard-on. That would be too embarrassing.

"Hi Britta," he said, slightly nervous. "How are you?"

Britta glanced briefly towards him before returning her concentration to the ground before her. "Fine, thanks."

For Jake, the silence that followed was awkward,

made all the worse by Elton whispering in his ear, "Shot down in flames."

A momentary flash of anger behind his eyes faded quickly, and he smiled, able to see the humour inherent in just about any situation. "Might see you later," he said as he and Elton turned and headed back out of the wood. They smiled and nodded at Scott as they passed him on his way back to the dig.

"I don't think she was exactly bowled over by your charms," said Elton, smiling, as they reached the road and turned towards Anbal village centre.

"Well," said Jake. "She's not my type anyway."

Further conversation was cut short as Jake's phone rang and he dragged it out of the back pocket of his jeans. Always wary of unexpected phone calls, he relaxed when he saw it was only Travis. "Hi, Travis. What's up?"

Travis's voice came through loud enough for Elton to lean close and hear. *"There's some strange shit going on at Dennis's house again. Weirder than last time."*

"You've got to let us in on this one, man. We missed out last time," said Elton, leaning even closer.

"That's why I'm ringing, dumbass! Dennis is convinced Swan is calling out to him from… somewhere."

"You mean like the spirit world?" said Jake, his excitement rising. He'd always wanted the chance to investigate like they did on TV—only seriously.

"I've no idea. But I do know I heard her myself. Or, at least, I think I did."

"Cool." Elton was smiling broadly.

"I need some ideas before Dennis does something crazy. So, I've come to you two. Give it some thought and let me know, okay?"

Jake didn't need time to think. "A seance."

"What?"

"Right," said Elton. "Classic way to contact spirits."

"Really?"

"Can you think of anything better?" said Jake.

There was a pause on the other end of the line, and Jake and Elton looked at each other, smiling. This was a chance they'd been waiting for.

A sudden barking and growling startled them. A dog was pulling away as its owner tried to enter Ottmor Wood. It continued to bark and bare its teeth with the low rumble of a growl, but an occasional whimper leaked through.

"Guess it doesn't want a walk today," said Elton, shrugging.

Jake said nothing. For a reason he could not identify, the behaviour of the dog unnerved him. He thought he recognised the dog and its owner as fairly regular walkers through the wood. Why wouldn't the dog go in there today? He felt a slight twist of anxiety in his stomach, which made no sense to him. He didn't even like dogs that much.

"Okay."

"What?"

Travis's voice on the phone dragged Jake away from his contemplation of the dog. He had forgotten for a moment that they were still talking.

"I said, 'Okay.' A seance it is. As long as I can persuade Dennis."

CHAPTER NINETEEN

Harvey Amos could not understand what was wrong with Buster, his dog. They often went through Ottmor Wood on their morning walk, and yet this morning Buster was refusing to go. He was barking, even showing some aggression, which Harvey also found unusual. Buster was such a quiet, well-behaved dog. Even compared to other adult Labradors, he was exceptionally calm and placid.

Until now.

"Come on, boy," said Harvey quietly, glancing up the road to the two men talking on a phone. "You're embarrassing me."

He supposed he could give up on the thought of going through Ottmor Wood, but Harvey was stubborn. It was his stubbornness, his refusal to accept anything but the best from people that had seen him into senior management at the Battens Brothers factory. He saw no reason to change just because he'd retired. Buster had to do as his master wanted. There was no room for negotiation.

With a final, more decisive tug, he dragged Buster onto the path that led through the centre of Ottmor Wood. Out of sight of others, he relaxed a little. He had never liked being embarrassed. It hurt his not inconsiderable pride.

"You and I need a long talk when we get home," he said to Buster.

Buster was now walking slowly, with an air of reluctance that transcended the species. The pleading eyes turned up to his master were equally universal. Harvey could not mistake the message, but years of management had hardened him to such displays. He had fired people whose first child was on the way, who were deep in debt and would lose their house if they lost their job, and many other sob stories. He had heard them all, and none of them affected his decision. He loved Buster, even more than he loved his bitter, sarcastic wife, but he would not give in to such a blatant emotional appeal.

"We are walking through this wood, whether you like it or not," he said. "Now, behave. Those archaeologist types will be up ahead, and I don't want you embarrassing me again!"

The area of ground Simon had been excavating was now at a depth that made further digging with the trowel difficult, if not impossible. Breathing heavily, he looked up at his two students, still scraping away in the proper, cautious method he taught on his field trips. That he had ignored his own teaching did not concern him. The

compulsion to dig downward, careless of any distur-
bance to possible artifacts, had been too strong to ignore. He didn't understand why, but neither did he
question it. It was important that the root was uncovered.
Another thing he didn't understand, but didn't question.

This stone and its root had become of prime impor-
tance to him, more so than any other find on any other
field trip, and he would not stop, despite the attitude of
his superiors at the university.

He hadn't told Britta and Scott yet, but he had
received an email from Professor Vance late last night.
The department did not consider the stone to be of
enough interest to justify spending any of the budget
on it. There would be no archaeological dig at the site.
At least, not one funded by the university. He had been
instructed to pack up and return. Something he had no
intention of doing.

Instead, he was shortcutting. Taking risks to reach
his goal quicker. Fuck the university. Fuck Vance. This
was *his* find. *Gjallarbru*. The bridge between the living
and the dead. It was the find of a lifetime, he was convinced of it. Uncovering the root was just the beginning.

A low growl interrupted his thoughts. A man he
vaguely recognised as a local, was standing on the nearby path, tugging on a dog lead. The dog had planted its
paws firmly on the ground and was staring at Simon,
teeth bared.

"I'm really sorry," the man was saying. "I don't
know what's got into Buster this morning. He's normally no problem with other people."

"Don't worry about it," said Simon, smiling. "Your
dog will walk on now."

Simon felt a sudden dizziness come over him, and
he placed a hand on the ground to steady himself. The

words were still in his head, but had he really said them? He couldn't remember actually speaking, saying anything, let alone that strange thing about the dog. His eyesight was a little blurred as he watched the dog reluctantly move away with its master, all the time looking back and baring its fangs. At that moment, in his disorientation and confusion, Simon hated the dog, and the man for bringing it here. He wished they could officially rope the site off, but he needed university backing for that. And he didn't have it.

He turned back to the hole he had dug and angrily thrust the trowel into it. The blade caught the root, slicing off a sliver no longer than his little finger, and no thicker than a leaf.

A sudden blast of thunder made Simon and his students flinch, ducking their heads in automatic response. Even Simon's usual forewarning had failed to detect the approach of this storm. The sky blackened rapidly as the wind rose. Heavy, driving rain pounded the ground, knocking leaves off trees and making the whole wood rustle and hiss.

"What the hell?"

Scott had jumped to his feet and was running for the Land Rover. Britta, with a quick look towards Simon, did the same.

Simon climbed slowly to his feet. He looked up, enjoying the feel of the rain splashing on his face. A jagged lance of lightning, the almost immediate explosion of thunder. He laughed as he walked slowly after his students. It was strange, but he felt no urge to run, to get out of the storm. Instead, he enjoyed it, revelled in it.

He looked at the sliver of root in his hand, accidentally cut off, and now his to keep. He could still feel the pulse of the root thumping through this small piece.

He could feel power of a kind he could not identify. But it was strong. And it was his.

The sudden storm had caught Harvey completely off guard. He could do nothing but turn up his collar, duck his head, and push towards home, dragging Buster behind him. It was quicker to head for the Wyatt Road entrance, and he hurried along the path, never running, but increasing his walking pace to the fastest he could manage.

Buster whimpered. The rain seemed to hit him harder than usual. The wind pushed and tugged with more ferocity. He had sensed something wrong with the whole wood, and especially with the human back there. And now that *wrongness* had become smothering in its thickness, its dead weight. He struggled against it, trying to keep up with his master.

Wyatt Road lay just ahead. Harvey could see the pavement and the houses. Not far to go. Then, up the road, out of the top, and home. Soon be there. He just wished Buster wouldn't drag his feet so much.

A blinding flash. A deafening boom. Lightning hit a tree to his left. He felt the searing heat, heard the clatter from above as an overhanging branch was sheared off. Harvey Amos looked up and managed a short scream before the jagged protrusion that had once sprouted leaves speared his left eye, popping it like a sludge-filled balloon. He fell, the back of his head hitting the ground hard, the following branch crushing his skull.

Buster ran, the fear in him greater than his loyalty to his master. He ran for the road and the houses he could see. He would be safe where humans lived.

He had reached the pavement when the lightning struck again.

The paving slab cracked, split down the middle. Buster was blown across the road to the other side, where his blackened, smoking carcass lay still, his smoldering lead trailing back towards Ottmor Wood.

CHAPTER TWENTY

Dennis saw the activity at the bottom of the road when he pulled the green wheelie bin to the end of the drive. Several police cars, an ambulance, and the entrance to Ottmor Wood taped off. Presumably, it was something to do with the unexpected storm that morning, but he wasn't overly interested. He didn't see how it affected him or his preparations for Swan's return. Nevertheless, he could not completely suppress a feeling of disquiet.

Back inside the house, he supported himself on the newel post at the base of the stairs. The pain in his back made standing straight a near impossibility. His knees would give way without warning, sending a stabbing pain through his legs. His hands ached, and the joints looked swollen. He needed to pause often to catch his breath. There was a pressure in his chest, and once or twice, warning pains jabbed across and down his left arm. But it was worth it.

The predominant smells in the house were polish, bleach, and floral air freshener. Gone were the musty, dirty, unwashed odours. Clothes had been washed or stuffed into black plastic sacks and thrown outside. The same with plates, cups, and pots and pans. He only kept what he needed, the rest was discarded. It was a clean sweep, a new beginning for him and the returning Swan.

Overnight, unable to sleep, worrying about Swan being held somewhere against her will, he had decided to discard the idea. Swan was coming home. That was the only interpretation he could accept.

A whisper in the air that turned into nothing but the breeze drifted through open windows.

For a moment he had hoped... but it had been quiet since he woke that morning.

He thought again of the activity down by Ottmor Wood, almost convinced there was a connection between whatever had happened and Swan's silence. But it was an elusive, possibly non-existent connection, and after a moment, he let it go. Why should there be a connection? Swan would talk to him again soon. She had to.

He longed for her voice, even buried in the sibilant whispers of the house. That one word, his name, had saved him. Swan had saved him. He no longer merely existed through each day, barely conscious of the passing hours, unmoving and uncaring. He had a purpose now, a reason to live. Swan was coming back, and he had finally transformed the house into something she would be happy with.

Sudden pain crushed his chest, causing him to clutch at it and double over. Losing his grip on the newel post, he slid down to sit on the bottom step. He felt cold, but knew his face was bathed with sweat. This was worse than when Swan called the ambulance, and he wondered whether this time it really *was* a heart attack.

But he couldn't die now. Not with Swan on her way back to him. It wouldn't be fair!

A police car blocked Travis from turning into Wyatt Road. As one of the two policemen seated inside climbed out and walked towards him, he wound down his window.

"What's going on?"

"Can I ask what your business on Wyatt Road is, sir?" said the policeman, politely but firmly.

"Visiting a sick friend," said Travis. "Is everything okay?"

"There's been a bit of an incident down by the wood, sir," said the policeman. "Nothing to worry about, but we don't want sightseers getting in the way. What's the name of your friend?"

"Dennis Parkes."

"And the house number?"

"Twenty."

The policeman turned to his colleague. Travis had no doubt his answers were being checked on their computer system. That didn't concern him, but he couldn't help wonder what the *bit of an incident* was. Was the team from the university that Jake and Elton had told him about involved? More importantly, were Jake and Elton involved?

He fought the urge to call them immediately, doubting that the police would be impressed if he suddenly pulled out his phone. But as soon as he reached Dennis's... *If* he reached Dennis's.

"That all checks out, sir," said the policeman, startling Travis from his worried thoughts. "You can go and visit your friend, but no further down the road. Understood?"

"Absolutely," said Travis, feeling certain his progress would be watched.

The police car reversed just enough to let him squeeze through, then moved back to block the road again as soon as he had passed.

He had an uneasy feeling as he drove slowly down the road. Perhaps it was just the presence of so many police and the white-suited forensic people he could see climbing over the stile and entering the wood, but he felt it was something more. Something much closer to him.

He parked outside Dennis's house, noted the black bin bags piled under the bay window, and rang the doorbell.

Dennis answered after a short delay, ushering him inside with a smile that, to Travis, seemed strained.

Without comment, Travis noted Dennis's grey pallor and a forehead speckled with sweat.

"What d'you think?" said Dennis, his good humour forced and false. "Good, yes?"

"Very clean and tidy," said Travis, looking more at his friend than the house. "You need to take it easy. You're not exactly built for this kind of intense activity."

"Well, I admit I had a bit of a scare just before you arrived. But I'm okay now."

"A bit of a scare?" Travis's brow furrowed, concerned. "What kind of scare? You look a little grey, Dennis."

"I'm fine. Just some chest pain, that's all."

"Did you take your spray?"

"Yes, I took the spray."

"And it worked?"

"Third time. But it worked."

Travis studied his friend's face carefully. It didn't look right. Something about the eyes, the lack of colour in the skin.

"Let's sit down," he said. "I'll make us a drink."

Minutes later, with Dennis sitting in his armchair and Travis perched on the edge of the settee, both with mugs of tea in their hands, Travis began to see the first sign of colour in Dennis's cheeks. He relaxed a little, feeling that any immediate danger to his friend's health had passed. Now it felt safe to talk about the main reason for his visit.

"I've been talking your whole situation over with Jake and Elton," he said.

Dennis smiled. It seemed a little weak to Travis.

"And what did the dynamic duo come up with?"

Travis hesitated, wondering whether now *was* a good time to bring this up. It was obvious Dennis was not completely over the recent angina attack. But, then again, he wondered whether it really made any difference at all. Dennis's reaction would no doubt be the same.

"They suggested we hold a seance."

Dennis almost spat out a mouthful of tea as he laughed. "A seance? Here? But Swan's not dead."

"I know, I know," said Travis, deciding this was not the time for a discussion on semantics and a definition of *dead*. "But she is speaking to you out of thin air, like some kind of spirit or ethereal being. They believe a seance will help you contact her properly, and allow her to say more than just your name."

"I haven't heard her at all for a while," said Dennis quietly, as though speaking to himself. "I do need to speak to her."

"I know it sounds like a daft idea," said Travis. "But I can't see any harm in it. And if it *should* work, then all the better. Right?"

"Do you believe they know what they're talking about?" Dennis chuckled to himself. "After all, this is Jake and Elton. I don't know them as well as you do, but they seemed more than a little *out there* when we met."

"They know about these kinds of things," said Travis. "It's one of their main interests. I believe they can pull this off." He only wished he was as confident as he sounded.

"Okay then," said Dennis with a smile. "On your recommendation, let's go ahead and do a seance. It'll be a bit of a laugh, if nothing else."

"I'll give them a call. Let them know to go ahead and make whatever preparations they need."

And check they weren't involved in whatever happened in Ottmor Wood.

CHAPTER TWENTY-ONE

The Deep Anchor was busy with early evening trade. Families out for tea mixed with hardened drinkers. Groups of people, barely old enough to drink, gathered in organically defined enclaves, drinking sparingly, trying to spread their money over what would be a long night. Sitting slightly apart, involved but unwittingly remote, were the designated drivers, sipping cola or lemonade, hiding slight resentment behind cheerful smiles and spattered conversation.

Jake and Elton, belonging to no social group but their own, eased their way through, heading straight for the bar. It took only a moment for Jake to spot Britta perched on a stool, cradling a glass of wine between her palms. Scott sat alongside her, but he barely registered in Jake's interest.

"Let's join Britta," said Jake over his shoulder to Elton.

Elton sighed. It wasn't the first time Jake's libido

had dictated their destination. He doubted it would be the last either.

"Just remember, we're here to meet Travis and make plans, not to get off with one of the archaeologists."

"It was your idea to meet in the pub," said Jake. "I'd have preferred outside somewhere. You know, not so noisy and crowded."

"After this morning, I feel safer indoors than out," said Elton. "With a good solid roof over my head."

Jake laughed and continued manoeuvring towards Britta and Scott.

"Look out, here come the local stoners," said Scott, muttering into his pint of beer.

Britta laughed. "Don't be so cruel. They seem harmless enough. And they called in this gig, so you should be grateful."

"Some gig. A man and his dog got killed today, a bit too close for comfort."

Britta's smile faded. "Shit happens. Although this was a bit close."

"Could have been us."

"But it wasn't," said Britta, looking up as Jake and Elton approached. "Just be thankful for that."

The smile returned to her face as Jake leaned onto the bar next to her, Elton just beyond him.

"Nice to see you again," she said. "This your local?"

"When we feel sociable, yes," said Jake, returning her smile. He glanced towards Scott, then quickly around the pub. "Your boss not with you tonight?"

"The professor prefers to stay in his room, working," said Scott.

"This is the first time we've been out in the evening." Britta sighed. "We needed a drink tonight."

"I'm not surprised," said Jake. "We heard about what happened in the wood. Did you see it?"

"No, thank God." Britta shuddered. "We saw the man and his dog go past us not long before, but we were busy running for cover from the storm."

"Weird, that storm," said Elton, quietly. "Almost unreal."

"We saw a man walking his dog going into the woods," said Jake, ignoring Elton. "Not sure it's the same one, but the dog didn't want to go."

"Knew something bad was going to happen," said Elton. "Animals can sense things."

"He's right," said Britta. "I have a dog, back home, not at the university. I'm sure she can sense when things are about to happen."

"You have a dog?" said Jake. "So, who's looking after it? Husband? Boyfriend?"

Britta laughed. "My parents. I don't have either of the other two."

"Hard to believe," said Jake, smiling.

"Maybe I'm just hard to please." Britta returned the smile.

Scott groaned, and when the others looked towards him, quickly raised his empty glass. "I need another drink."

"I'll get it," said Jake. "Lager?"

Scott nodded, ignoring the challenge in Britta's glare. If she wanted to flirt in an overly obvious manner, that was her business, but it didn't mean he had to like it.

"You want another?" Jake pointed to Britta's half-full glass of white wine.

"Yes, thanks. Medium." Britta turned from Scott back to Jake, her smile returning. "So, you two out on your own tonight?"

While Jake caught the eye of Frank, the owner of The Deep Anchor, and ordered drinks for all four of them, Elton took up the conversation.

"We're meeting a friend. Travis Newman. Should be along soon." He hesitated, and then added, "You'll like him. He's nice."

To Britta, it seemed like an odd thing to say. But there was a lot about Elton that was odd. Jake, too, for that matter, but not quite so much. Plus Jake was kind of cute, and his obvious liking for her made it fun to flirt. Elton didn't seem the flirting type. She wasn't at all sure what *type* Elton was. She couldn't read him. But she did know he wasn't *her* type.

For a moment she thought of Simon, alone in his room, presumably working, as he said he would be. She surprised herself by feeling grateful for his absence. Some part of her said he would have been a liability with the younger men around, perhaps even an embarrassment. Not because of his age, but because of the way he looked at her, the way she knew he felt. She suspected that, with a few beers inside him, he could become jealous of the attention of, for example, Jake. And he certainly would not have appreciated her flirting. It was more fun, more relaxed, without him there, and not just because he was her professor. She glanced at Scott and wondered if he felt the same. Or did he secretly wish Simon was there with them, for exactly the same reasons she was glad he wasn't?

The pub door opened, distracting her. The man who walked in made her forget about Simon, Scott, and Elton. He even made her forget about flirting with

Jake. Here was a man who, she knew immediately, *was* her type. Very much so.

She watched him pause just inside the door, scanning the room for somebody. Was it wrong that she hoped it wasn't a girlfriend or, even worse, a wife? She felt a shiver of excitement in her stomach as the man looked her way. Was it her imagination, or did his gaze linger a second longer on her than on others? She liked to think so.

Jake turned from the bar and handed her a glass of wine, which she took without thinking. He was about to turn back and collect more drinks when he saw the new arrival. Britta could hardly believe it when he raised his hand, beckoning the stranger over.

This must be Jake and Elton's friend, she thought, barely suppressing a smile. *I'm beginning to like it here.*

Jake felt any chance he had with Britta slipping away the moment he introduced Travis to the two archaeology students. The attraction between Travis and Britta was so obvious it was almost cliché. It was a wonder a violinist hadn't appeared from out of the growing crowd of drinkers to serenade them. But Jake was a realist regarding his chances with women. He enjoyed flirting, but he never really expected it to progress much further. And if he had to lose to anyone, at least Travis was a friend and a worthy winner.

Travis was telling Britta and Scott about Dennis's experiences, and about the seance they intended to hold.

"Can I come along?" said Britta. "I've never taken part in a seance. It sounds interesting."

Travis looked towards Jake. "Do numbers matter?"

"I don't think so," said Jake. "But everyone has to take it seriously, otherwise it won't work."

"I wouldn't fool around," said Britta. "It really does interest me."

"What about you?" said Travis, talking across Britta to Scott.

"Me?" Scott seemed surprised to be invited. "I guess so. Yes. Sure. Why not?"

"Great," said Travis. "I just need to finalise the time with Dennis, and then I'll let you know. Where's best to get in touch?"

"Give me your phone," said Britta.

Travis handed his phone over, smiling as Britta typed on it.

"There," she said, handing the phone back. "I've added my number to your contacts. Just give me a ring when it's all sorted. Okay?"

"Perfect," said Travis.

Jake shrugged. Trust Travis to get her number without even trying. But at least he'd see her again at the seance. Maybe they should ask Alison along, too?

But what if Scott gets off with her?

The thought surprised and confused him, more so because of the intense feeling of jealousy that accompanied it. When they were younger, Alison had had boyfriends, he was certain. It hadn't bothered him then, so why now? Damn it, life was difficult. He needed some time alone to think it all through before things got too complicated.

CHAPTER TWENTY-TWO

In his Travelodge room, with the curtains closed and only the bedside lamps on, Simon Forrester sat on the edge of the bed and stared at the sliver of root in his hand.

Was it his fault that the man and the dog had been killed? Had he somehow wished it to happen, through some power in this small piece of root? It was hard to believe it possible, and yet the coincidence was too much for him to comfortably accept. In that moment, just before it happened, he had hated the man and his dog. And it was their fault that he cut the sliver of root.

He held the piece tightly, still feeling the pulse of the main root running through it. He might have cut it free, but it still belonged to its parent. It remained a part of the greater whole. The root had power. This sliver had power. The whole dig had turned both frightening and fascinating. The stone marked as *Gjallarbru*, the bridge between the living and the dead. A powerful living root attached to the stone. No, more than that. The root grew *out* of the stone.

He paused in his thought, an insight worming its way into his brain.

What if the root doesn't grow out of the stone? What if the stone grows out of the root?

And the root seemed never-ending. As deep as they could dig, it continued deeper.

Perhaps it has *no end,* he thought, smiling. *What if it grows out from something far larger than the stone? What if it is a root from* Yggdrasil?

Simon understood the flexibility of mythology and the slim connection to reality in all of the stories surrounding ancient society. How could they be factual when there were conflicting myths on all sides? History was written by the winners, mythology by the most popular. But now, for the first time, he began to believe that he should take at least some myths more literally. He seemed to have the evidence in front of him. A sliver from *Yggdrasil*, the Norse tree of life!

And with that revelation came the knowledge that he must return the sliver to its source. It was his task to make *Yggdrasil* whole once more.

Dennis had declined the invitation to the pub. He did not yet feel able to socialise, and certainly not out in a public place. He was already growing nervous about the seance idea, and the fact that it meant people coming to his house. Travis was the only person he felt truly comfortable with. And there was Swan, of course. Before she left. Looking forward to just being with her again was one of the things that kept him going.

The seance. The suggestion that a dubious ritual used to contact the dead could be used to contact Swan bothered him. Did they think Swan was dead? Travis had insisted not, but Dennis wasn't sure he believed him. They thought Swan was dead, and this seance would allow him to talk to her and find this out. Was that the secret, underlying reason behind all this? To convince him of Swan's death?

Swan is not *dead. She is alive and somehow contacting me through the ether, or the spiritual dimension, or the astral plane, or whatever! I don't understand it, but I know she's alive. She has to be.*

Occasionally he had doubts. Just after Travis left, he had doubts. Maybe Travis was right? Maybe he was deluding himself? Maybe there was nothing there at all, and it was all inside his head?

After Swan left, he thought he was going insane. The spiral down into the deepest depression he had ever experienced was frightening and unstoppable. Without Swan, he had no life. He would remain housebound until he died. The sooner, the better.

Memories of those dark days, such a short time ago, still haunted him at times. But he had pulled himself out. Just the one whispered word, the single thread of hope, had been enough to change his whole outlook. Life was worth living again. The house was worth cleaning. Swan was coming back.

Travis and the others disagreed. None of them would say it directly to his face, even Travis had backtracked, but they were certain Swan was dead and was never coming back.

Could they be right?

A wind, rising from nothing in the stillness of the front room, tugged at his clothes as though urging him to stand.

He looked for open windows, but could see none. He was more pleased than concerned. Things had been quiet with the strange phenomena recently, and he wanted to hear Swan's voice again calling his name.

The wind strengthened until he felt it swirling a-round his back, under his buttocks, trying to lift him from the armchair. It roared its insistence, tugging and swirling until Dennis finally acquiesced and stood.

The armchair moved, pushed across the floor by a sudden gust, and for the first time, Dennis felt a little afraid. Anything loose on tabletops or window ledges flew through the air, past Dennis, and towards the far wall. Photo frames ricocheted off his raised arms and clattered against the plaster. A candlestick, retrieved from the back of a cupboard in the hope of a romantic atmosphere once Swan was back, span past his head and he heard a *thunk*!

He turned and stared at the candlestick, jutting out from a hole it had punched in the wall.

This is getting dangerous!

He leaned into the wind, pushing his way towards the door and out into the hallway. The wind still moved through into the kitchen and up the stairs, but without the ferocity of the front room. Dennis was about to think he could maybe relax a little when the whispering began.

It was not Swan, not this time. Many voices hissed and slithered, twisting around each other, overlapping, turning what might have been intelligible language into gibberish. He knew they said words, but he had no idea what those words were.

From the corner of his eye, he saw shadows drifting down the stairs. Others moving in the kitchen. The whispering grew louder, the shadows moved quicker. Somehow it conveyed the impression to Dennis that they were agitated. Either something was wrong, or something exciting was happening. Whichever, the entities, spirits, call-them-what-you-will, were in an uproar.

This time the Stygian blackness bled upwards from the floor. A void. A hole, tempting Dennis to fall inside. And then the eyes. The sudden opening. The staring.

Dennis did not run. Despite his fear, he stood his ground and looked into the emptiness, and the emptiness mocked him. He could feel it. Laughing. Taunting. When he dared to look directly into the eyes, he saw nothing but contempt.

Slowly, the dark truth strangled his hope. The unspoken message from the blackness crushed his spirit, and he knew that, in his mind, he was spiralling into an even darker hole than the one before him.

Swan *was* dead!

There was no longer any doubt. She had been swallowed by the same hole, the same rent in the fabric of reality that faced him. Then it had waited, raising his hopes with teasing whispers using her voice. Made him feel there was something to live for after all, only to destroy him, now, with the truth. It was cruel and vicious. It had played a game where only it knew the rules, and it had killed him as surely as it had killed Swan.

What was the point in carrying on? What was there to look forward to? To hope for? To live for? Without Swan, his life was nothing. It was empty, a void of depression and misery. Without Swan, he ceased to exist. He was worthless.

With tears running down his cheeks, he closed his eyes and stepped into the blackness.

Alison made a conscious effort to not look into any mirrors. She knew she would not like what she saw. In particular, the smudged makeup and the puffy, red eyes would remind her that she'd been crying. She didn't want that.

Edgar Leonard, a partner in Leonard & Ford Accountants, and the focus of Alison's adoration and love, had brought his wife to the office that morning. She was pretty, immaculately dressed and constantly smiling, looking very comfortable, very *happy* alongside her husband.

Alison hated her.

It was unreasonable, unfounded hate, but it was hate. A hate full of envy and jealousy, of bitterness and self-criticism. How could she compete with this sophisticated older woman? How could she ever persuade Edgar to leave a wife he seemed, on the surface at least, to love?

She thought something moved in the far corner of the apartment, seen out of the corner of her eye, but when she turned to look, there was nothing.

Was that a voice? A whisper coming from somewhere behind her?

Again she turned. Again there was nothing.

"Elton? Jake? If you're pissing around, I'll kill you!"

But she knew Elton and Jake were out, down at the pub. They wouldn't be back for some time. So, who was whispering?

She thought the first whisper had come, perhaps, from one of the bedrooms, but when it started up again, it was in the air all around her. And not just one voice, but several.

As she turned, looking for anything that might be the source of the strange sounds, she saw more fleeting movement from the corner of her eye. Shadows shifting in corners. Half-seen shapes skittering across the floor by her feet, making her jump back.

"What do you want?" she shouted, her voice barely audible above the growing susurration of hissing whispers. "Leave me alone!"

She raised her hands to her face and felt wetness. She was crying again. She hadn't even noticed.

The myriad of whispering voices began to coalesce, merging together until the noise became almost intelligible speech. Despite her confusion and fear, Alison found herself straining to hear, to understand. The shadowy shapes continued to dart in and out of her peripheral vision, but she ignored them, focusing fully on the voice.

Finally, as the last of the whispers melted into the one, she understood what was being said. Just one word.

Alison.

The voice fell silent, the shadows grew still. Alison stood in the middle of the apartment, breathing heavily, her face streaked with dried tears. She was no longer confused, no longer frightened. It was all so clear now. The voices and shadows had made her understand what she needed to do.

What could she offer Edgar to tempt him away from his perfect wife? Every fantasy, every perversion he had ever dreamed of. She would fuck him in ways that would have him begging for more. She could see it in her head, a vision of brutal, uncontrolled sex. She felt her nipples harden. Fingers that seemed barely under her power crept to the wetness between her legs.

The intensity crashed, desire and fantasy falling from

her as though a sheet of darkness had been dragged away. How could she think such things of Edgar? Her love for him was pure, uncontaminated by the base needs of the body. She would steal him away through her love, not through sex.

She pulled her hand away from her thighs, the fingers glistening wetly in the overhead light. It made her feel ill. Moving quickly to the kitchen, she rinsed them clean under the tap.

What had happened? There were things moving in the apartment, and people whispering. Invisible people. But none of that made sense. And then those terrible thoughts as the voice spoke her name. Was she going mad? Had she imagined the whole thing?

It was clear to her as she splashed cold water onto her face, trying to shock herself into rationality, that there was no way she was staying alone in the apartment for the rest of the evening. Elton and Jake were at the pub? It would not take her long to get dressed and hurry down there.

The police tape had been taken down. A single piece remained, stuck firmly to the fence post by the entrance to Ottmor Wood. It fluttered in the brisk breeze, like a small bird struggling to fly.

Simon Forrester stared at it until he was satisfied it could do him no harm.

A strangely heightened awareness had descended on him as he left the Travelodge. An awareness of danger all around, from both the animate and the inanimate. He held the sliver of root close to his chest as he walked. It was important he not lose it, and that no one should take it away from him. He was the carrier, the one who was tasked to return the sliver to the root.

Now, with one final look around the deserted roadway, he ducked into Ottmor Wood.

The wind strengthened as he tramped along the muddy path. With it came sharp needles of rain, stabbing his face, his eyes. He struggled on, barely able to see, but never doubting he was heading in the right direction. The sliver of root grew warm in his hands, and he knew he was nearing *Gjallarbru*.

He stumbled over the rock in his eagerness to reach it, falling heavily onto the ground.

Not bothering to try and stand, he wriggled forward towards the hole they had dug under the rock. Scooping handfuls of mud and rainwater with one hand, he cleared the hole of accumulated debris and dug deeper. Fingers bled, a fingernail ripped in two, but he kept digging with one hand, the other grasping the sliver of root. He passed the part of the root from where the sliver had been inadvertently sliced, but kept going. Something urged him to dig as deep as he could.

The muffled sound of running water finally stopped him. Breathing heavily from the exertion, his hands and face streaked and splattered with mud, he lay half in the hole and listened. Somewhere far below, underground, there was running water. And not just a trickle, but a full-flowing river.

Simon Forrester, scientist and practical man, began to laugh, somewhere between joy and madness. First had been the discovery of *Gjallarbru*, the bridge between the worlds of the living and the dead. Then there had been a root of *Yggdrasil*, the tree of life. And now it seemed he was close to uncovering *Gioll*, the river that divided the worlds of the living and the dead, the river bridged by *Gjallarbru*.

It seemed nonsense, the kind of simplistic idiocy he berated the more foolish of his students over. The Norse tales were *mythology*. They were not history, and the places they inhabited were not real! Yet he was convinced that evidence to the contrary was there in front of him. He believed in the mythology. He believed in the truth, the validity of that world. And he had uncovered its resting place.

He pressed the sliver back into the root, healing the wound.

The sky darkened, the rain grew hard and heavy, and darting shadows, half-seen shapes, moved among the trees of Ottmor Wood. They whispered. Sibilant, hissing, serpent-like. One word. One name. He knew what he must do.

Britta!

CHAPTER TWENTY-THREE

Travis was relaxed talking to Britta. In some organic way, the others had drifted slightly aside, leaving the two of them more or less alone. Only Scott hung around the periphery, unwilling to move far from his student colleague.

This girl, this student who was undoubtedly smarter than him, fascinated Travis. She was stunning to look at, that was the first thing he noticed as he entered the pub. Like the many cheesy movies he had seen, it was as though a spotlight had picked her out of the crowd. And when she returned the look and their eyes made contact... He could almost hear the soaring violins.

The fantasy had persisted until he actually got to talk to her. Then she became a person, and all the more attractive for it. She was smart, she was funny. He quickly felt almost as relaxed talking to her as he did when talking to Jake or Elton, or Dennis, before Swan's disappearance. Almost. He could never quite forget her physicality, the face, the hair, the body. It kept him slightly off balance, slightly more self-aware than he would have been with his old friends. He couldn't help but analyse every word and movement he made for how it might look to her. He wanted to impress her. He wanted her to *like* him. It made complete relaxation impossible, but it made it all the more exciting.

He imagined leaning in towards her, their arms slipping around each other. Kissing. Fondling.

"Sometimes you seem to go off somewhere, in your mind," said Britta, breaking the spell, which Travis was not sorry for. "I can see your eyes defocus."

"Bad habit," he said. "Lots of things going 'round in my head."

"Such as?"

"Oh, the usual stuff," he said, floundering a little. "Work, money, worrying about my friend, Dennis…"

She smiled, dropping her voice to a whisper, and leaning forward. "That's a pity," she said. "I was hoping you might be thinking about me."

Travis laughed awkwardly and knew he was blushing. He could feel the heat in his cheeks. This was unfamiliar ground. He couldn't remember the last time he'd blushed.

Britta dropped a hand onto his arm. Her laugh was easy, relaxed. "I do believe you were," she said. "I'm glad, 'cause I was thinking about you."

Travis was aware of Scott's eyes trying to bore into him, his disapproval at the turn in the conversation obvious. But he was not part of it, and Travis felt no guilt at ignoring him.

"I'm glad, too," he said, feeling it a little weak, but unable to conjure anything better at the moment. His insides were knotting, twisting, but it was a good feeling. He searched for something to say, finding a genuine interest among the throwaway, unworthy lines of small-talk that cluttered his mind. "Britta's a nice name," he said, hoping it didn't sound too contrived. "I don't think I've ever met someone called Britta before. Not English?"

If Britta seemed in any way disappointed at the turn in the conversation, she didn't show it. Instead, she nodded and continued to smile. "Scandinavian. It was my mother's choice. I think it reminded her of her family's roots."

"Like Swan," said Travis. "Dennis's wife. Her full name's Swanhilde, and her maiden name was Bergelmir, I think. That's Scandinavian, isn't it?"

"I'd say so. I wish I could have met her."

Travis nodded, but with talking about Swan, his thoughts had returned to Dennis.

Britta seemed to read his mind. "I bet you're worried about your friend," she said, straightening in her seat, her manner shifting from frivolous to sympathetic without hesitation. "I picked up a little of what's been going on from Jake and Elton. You should give Dennis a call. Just to put your mind at rest."

Travis smiled and nodded. She was right. He would not be able to completely put Dennis out of his mind until he had satisfied himself that his old friend was okay.

"Just a quick call," he said, already selecting Dennis's number from his contacts. "Won't be a moment."

He watched Britta turn and exchange a few quiet words with Scott while the phone rang. He admired the way she made that effort to include her colleague. So many women would have brushed him off and stranded him once her interest was taken elsewhere.

The phone continued to ring.

Britta took a sip of her drink, turned, and smiled at Travis before once again sharing a few words with a happier looking Scott.

There's pleasure in simply watching her move, thought Travis. *I've never met a woman like this before.*

"Come on, Dennis," he grumbled to himself, becoming impatient, wanting to get back to Britta. "Pick up."

The phone continued to ring.

"No answer?" said Britta.

Travis shook his head, his impatience turning to worry. Perhaps Dennis was asleep? But Travis knew that Dennis slept lightly these days, waking at the hint of a whisper in the house. He would certainly not sleep through the ringing of his phone.

"Something's wrong," he said. "Dennis would pick up when he saw it was me. He wouldn't ignore it."

"We should go round and check on him," said Britta. "Just in case something's happened."

"We?" Travis finished the unanswered call and returned the phone to his pocket.

"That's if you don't mind me coming along? I know I don't know Dennis, but I know you, and I don't like to see you so worried. I'd be happier if I were there to see your mind put at rest."

Travis could feel the genuineness of her concern, and it touched him. They had only just met and already she cared.

Jake watched Travis and Britta heading for the door and returned Travis's wave.

"Where are they going?" said Elton. "Or is it not polite to ask?"

Jake smiled. "It's not what you think. Travis was trying to call Dennis by the look of it. I think they've gone off to see why he didn't pick up."

"But why's *she* going?" said Elton, the beer helping to make his thoughts confused, unclear.

"It's a boy, girl thing," said Jake, quietly laughing. "You wouldn't understand."

"Very funny, asshole."

"Watch your language, dipshit."

Elton was about to come back with another casual insult when he saw his sister, Alison, push her way into the pub. The distressed look on her face, and the way she anxiously scanned the bar until she saw him, was worrying.

Jake had also seen her entrance, and also noted her unusually worried expression. "Alison," he said as she joined them at the bar. "Is everything okay?"

"You look worried, big sister," said Elton. "What's wrong?"

Alison ignored their questions. "I've come out without any money," she said, her voice strained, tightly controlled.

"No problem," said Jake. "I can buy you a drink or three, but why not tell us what's going on?"

Alison looked from Jake to her brother, and then to the surface of the bar in front of her. "I don't want to talk about it," she said. "I just need to be here with you two idiots, okay?" She forced a smile. "I don't want to be on my own at the moment."

"No problem," said Jake, masking his worry with a smile and a wave to the bartender.

"My big sister is always welcome," said Elton, a little slurred.

Alison seemed to relax as a drink was placed in front of her. She sat between Jake and Elton and showed no sign that she wanted to move anytime soon. Jake was more than happy to have her there, but he couldn't stop thinking about what might have happened to scare her into coming.

Had it not been for the ever-present anxiety about Travis's friend, the walk from the pub to Wyatt Road would have been a pleasant experience, thought Britta. Instead, every step brought more worry, more speculation. She could almost see the thoughts as they swept over Travis's face, each one darkening his expression a little more. There was no conversation between them, and she understood Travis's need to concentrate on the matter in hand. This was no time for small talk, or even things of a more personal, and more serious, note. She was there as support for Travis. That had been her sole reason for coming along. It had surprised her almost as much as it seemed to surprise Travis.

There was no police presence on Wyatt Road now. The scene had been forensically examined, evidence bagged, people questioned. The final judgement by the local coroner would almost certainly be accidental death. What else could it be? Just a man and his dog, unlucky to be in the wrong two places at the wrong times. It was impossible that the lightning could have been striking deliberately at them, even though both the strike on the tree and the one on the dog were perfect shots. Just bad luck.

Still, it made her a little uneasy as they walked down the road to number 20.

The house was dark, no light bleeding from the sides of curtains, or illuminating the bottled glass window in the front door.

"Dennis wouldn't sit in the dark," said Travis quietly, as though afraid to disturb the heavy silence that lay, almost palpably, on the house and its grounds. "He likes the light, keeping the house welcoming for when Swan comes home."

"Do you really think she's just going to turn up after all this time?" said Britta, her own voice matching Travis's in softness.

"I don't, but Dennis does."

"Jake said he hears her calling him."

"He does." Travis shrugged. "He's been through a lot."

"What do *you* believe?"

Travis shook his head, slowly. "I don't know."

They squeezed past the two parked and unused cars in the driveway. Without hesitation, Travis knocked on the front door. Lightly, at first, then harder when no one answered.

"What do you want to do?" said Britta, feeling strangely unsettled.

It's just a house. What's the matter with me? Don't want to appear all weak and frightened in front of Travis. I like him too much to screw things up like that.

"I have a key," said Travis. "You don't have to come in if you don't want to. I mean, I'm sure there's nothing there, but, you know…"

"I'm fine," said Britta, forcing a smile. "And I'm not letting you go in there on your own."

Travis unlocked the door and pushed inside. He reached for the switch, bringing light to the hallway, as he called, "Dennis? It's me, Travis. Where are you?"

There was no answer other than the slight echo thrown by empty rooms.

It feels deserted, thought Britta. *Travis's friend isn't here, I'm sure of it. No one is, except us.*

Travis was quickly checking the living room, the kitchen. He returned to Britta in the hallway, his expression confused and anxious. "I'm just going to look upstairs," he said. "Maybe you should stay here, just in case."

"In case of what?"

Travis hesitated before shaking his head. "I've no idea. I realise I'm probably being all very melodramatic, but I'm worried. You don't know Dennis. You don't know how weird things have been."

"Okay," said Britta, forcing a smile. "Go check upstairs and I'll wait here. But don't be too long."

It's only an empty house. Don't creep yourself out.

Travis smiled. "Be as quick as I can."

Britta watched him hurry up the stairs and could hear him moving from room to room. Other than the sound of Travis's searching, the house remained silent.

At least for a short while.

A faint hissing, right on the edge of her hearing, had Britta turning back and forth, trying to detect the direction the sound came from. Could it be a gas leak? Should she be worried? It grew in volume gradually, almost undetectably, starting as an indistinct hiss, becoming a rolling sibilance that suggested whispering, although any words were indistinguishable from the white noise behind them.

Despite an emptiness in her stomach and a tensing of muscles ready for flight, Britta was surprised to realise she wasn't scared. More curious, intrigued, but wary. Was this what Jake meant when he said Dennis heard voices? It was easy to see how someone with an already slender hold on reality might interpret the sounds as speech, hearing the words they wanted to hear. Even *she* felt, at times, that recognisable speech was a hair's breadth away in the undulating noise that now seemed to fill the hallway. But that was nonsense. There had to be rational, scientific explanation for the phenomena.

Although distracted by the sounds, she saw Travis coming back down the stairs. He was alone. Britta was not surprised. But she *was* surprised by the look of fear, almost panic on his face.

"Can you hear that?" he said, almost shouting to be heard. "That noise? That whispering!"

"Of course I can hear it," she said. "But it's not whispering. It can't be. We need to find where it's coming from."

The noise rose in sudden crescendo. The front door to the house flew open, making both Britta and Travis jump. The sharp breaking of glass cut through the hiss as the kitchen window, visible from the hallway, shattered.

The noise stopped, the sudden silence roaring in Britta's ears.

A single, recognisable word, hung in the air, a trace left by the noise.

"Travis!"

"Not possible," said Britta, shaking in the aftermath of the noise and the violent opening of the door so close to her. "It's just my mind trying to find a recognisable pattern."

"I used to think that," said Travis.

"But you can't believe anything else, can you?" said Britta, not sounding fully convinced herself. "There has to be a logical, *rational* explanation. I'll admit there's something going on in this house, but I can't believe it's anything supernatural."

"What did you hear?"

"When?"

"As the noise stopped," said Travis. "What *recognisable pattern* did your mind come up with?"

"I don't see that's relevant…"

"Was it my name?" Travis cut in, smiling grimly. "I'm betting it was."

Britta hesitated before answering, her eyes pulled towards the stairs as she thought she saw something move. Something dark. A shadow perhaps. There was nothing there. "Coincidence," she said. "Did you find your friend upstairs?"

Change the subject. I don't understand what's going on, and I'm afraid he'll convince me I'm wrong about it all.

"No," said Travis, shaking his head. "Dennis is not here."

"Maybe he just popped out?"

Bring the conversation 'round to more mundane things and get out of this house as soon as you can.

"Not Dennis."

Travis pulled his phone from his pocket.

"Who are you calling?" said Britta, her heart skipping as something dark skittered across the floor in her peripheral vision. She forced herself not to turn and stare, knowing, logically, that there would be nothing there.

"I'm calling Jake," said Travis. "You see, there's one thing you won't have been to able to recognise in that voice calling my name. It was Dennis's."

"Travis…"

"I know how mad that sounds," said Travis, interrupting. "And obviously you can leave at any moment. But I hope you'll stay. I hope you'll trust me."

Britta said nothing for a moment, staring at Travis as he stood, looking drawn, worried, and a little scared, his phone halfway to his ear, but not yet dialled. She felt a stirring inside, a flutter in her stomach. She cared about this man she had only just met. She cared and, yes, she did trust him, however ridiculous things might get. She wasn't entirely sure what she felt, but she knew it was powerful and gave her little choice but to stay.

"I trust you," she said. "But what are you going to tell Jake?"

"Whatever happened to Swan has happened to Dennis," said Travis. "It's time we had that seance!"

CHAPTER TWENTY-FOUR

Travis, Jake, and Elton dragged the table through from Dennis's kitchen into the living room.

"There's more space in here," said Travis as he stepped back and smiled at Britta. "I guess it's not ideal, but it's the best we can manage."

"There's nothing *ideal* about any of this," said Jake, dusting himself off. "To perform a seance, you're meant to have believers sitting around the table. People who are friendly towards the spirit world." He laughed. "Instead, we have a room full of sceptics, including myself and Elton."

"Shouldn't there be a medium or something?" said Scott from the doorway.

"It would've been nice," said Jake. "But none of us know one. It's not a necessity, from what I've read, but it's usually recommended."

"We'll manage," said Elton. "We always do."

"Have you done a lot of seances, then?" said Britta.

"None," said Elton, smiling. "This will be our first."

Alison eased herself past Scott and handed cups of tea to Travis and Britta. "We may all be crazy for being here," she said. "But at least we can be civilised. Anyone else want tea or coffee?"

"Tea, please," said Jake, smiling at Alison. "You know, I didn't think you'd come along. You normally run away the moment me and Elton start messing with anything unusual."

"I don't run away!" said Alison sharply. "I just don't choose to waste my life meddling in the ridiculous and the stupid, which is what you two mostly end up with."

"But you're here now."

"Yes, well," Alison faltered, not wanting to give her true reason for being there with them all. She was too frightened to go home and be alone. Whatever had happened earlier might just happen again. "I thought it was time to see what my little brother was up to. Keep an eye on him."

It was obvious to everyone that Elton was working towards a reply when Jake cut in, effectively disarming his friend.

"The atmosphere needs to be calm and uncluttered for this to work. Alison, why don't you just sit down for a moment, and *I'll* get the cups of tea."

He pulled one of the kitchen chairs away from the table and guided Alison to it, his arm round her waist.

Alison sat, feeling an odd tingle as Jake's hand lingered on her waist for longer than seemed necessary. She watched him leave and head for the kitchen, squeezing past Scott as he did so. Scott and Jake were so different, and yet both attractive in their own way. Jake's *way* might be a little wilder than most, but the attraction was still there. Her problem was that she had no idea whether these were her true thoughts or some after-effect of her strange experience.

After-effect or not, it was obvious that Scott liked her. The way his eyes kept sliding back to her, jerking away the moment he realised she was watching. Jake, on the other hand, she could not imagine him ever seeing her other than Elton's big sister and family friend. If her feelings continued to churn, her emotions sparking wildly, she would have to go for Scott. His positive response was a given.

"Do you have to be so obvious?" Elton had moved closer to her while she was thinking and now hissed in her ear. "You're behaving like some slut! Eyeing up that student, and Jake, too." He paused, seemed to gather his strength. "Stay away from Jake," he whispered vehemently. "Jake's... a friend."

Alison, feeling an unreasonable anger growing, and suddenly eager to retaliate, jumped on the inadvertent hesitation. "Are you sure you meant to say *friend*? Is there something you want to tell me, *little* brother?"

"There's nothing to tell," said Elton, his face flushed. "And if there was, you're the last person I would confess to. Just stop behaving like some common tramp!"

He stepped away as Jake re-entered the room carrying cups of tea and coffee.

Alison did not move, but to her surprise, the anger she felt seemed to add to the sexual desire and need that bubbled below her barely controlled surface. While not as strong as earlier, in her own apartment, it was increasingly difficult to suppress. She hoped she could hold out long enough to finish the seance. She had no wish to leave on her own.

The table was set with four candles they'd found in Dennis's kitchen drawers and a plain tablecloth. The light was off, the curtains closed, and the candlelight flickered in a slight breeze that wound through the room and around the sitters. There had not been enough kitchen chairs, and others had been carried down from upstairs to make up the numbers.

Jake sat at the head of the table, the others evenly spaced around. On his left sat Elton, then Britta, Travis, Scott, and finally, on his right, Alison.

"Shouldn't we have a Ouija board or something?" said Scott in a whisper, the darkened room seeming an inappropriate place for loud voices.

"Might have been useful," said Elton, also in a whisper. "But it's not necessary. And anyway, we don't have one."

His tone of voice suggested Scott was stupid to ask the question, and Jake did not miss the antagonism from Elton towards the student. If Scott noticed, he ignored it.

"Is everyone ready?" said Jake, his voice barely louder than Scott and Elton's, as though the candlelight and shadows dampened any thought of shouting.

A series of nods gave him his answer.

"If you'll all join hands, then we'll get this seance started."

As hands were joined, Jake took a deep breath, letting it out slowly, trying to calm the flutter of nerves in his stomach. He closed his eyes, feeling a strong grip from Alison on one side, and the slightly sweaty palm of Elton on the other.

"We gather tonight in the hope that any spirits within this house will give us a sign of their presence. You are welcome within our circle. We also ask for protecttion from any evil or angry spirits, wanting to communicate only with the well-intentioned. Please, join us when you are ready."

"How does he know about all this?" said Britta to Travis.

Elton, overhearing the question, whispered, "wiki-How," and a light laugh trickled around the table.

"Please forgive the frivolous nature of some of those gathered." Jake opened one eye, glaring at Elton, and then returned to his concentration. "We truly wish to communicate. We mean you no harm."

It could have been his imagination, but Jake thought the breeze quickened. A fluttering from the candles seemed to agree.

Somewhere in the house, a door slammed, the sudden noise making everyone around the table jump. Britta squeezed Travis's hand hard.

"If that's you," said Jake, recovering well, "then please join us in the circle. Don't be afraid."

Although the breeze did not strengthen, the curtains billowed, settling slowly back against the window frame.

"Fuck me," hissed Jake before gathering his shaken composure.

Travis, gripping Britta's hand almost as tightly as she gripped his, spoke. "Dennis? Swan? Is that you?"

"And if it is, stop dicking around!"

This came from Alison, and everyone looked at her in surprise.

"What?" she said. "I want to see some real action here tonight. Not just a slamming door and a bit of curtain blowing."

Elton was confused and a little frightened. He had

144

never heard Alison like this before. She could be annoying, exasperating even, but when in company, she always behaved impeccably. He felt he should say something, but had no idea what.

Scott felt Alison's finger stray from his palm and stroke down his thumb to his wrist. It made him both nervous and excited.

"Shall we get on with it, then?" said Alison, a slight sneer on her face. "Let's see what these fuckers can really do!"

"I don't think we can continue like this," said Jake a little nervously. "We need a calm atmosphere."

Alison let go of his hand and turned to Scott. "In that case, why don't you and me get out of here and go somewhere to fuck?"

Scott looked stunned as Alison stood and almost dragged him from his chair.

"Scott?" Britta also stood, having let go of Elton's hand. She still clung to Travis.

"Too late, dear," said Alison, laughing. "He's mine, at least for the next few minutes. You can have him afterwards." She paused, and her eyes caressed Britta's body so intimately that the younger girl felt uneasy. "And after that, I may just take a shot at you."

Alison dragged Scott from the room, although his protests were minimal. His inhibitions seemed stripped away the moment she pulled him from the chair.

The others watched them leave, too stunned to know what to do. They heard Alison call back to them, "If anyone wants to watch, we'll be in the kitchen."

"What the hell just happened?" said Travis after a moment of silence in the room. "What's going on?"

"That's not Alison," said Elton, almost in tears. "I don't know who it is, but it's not Alison!"

145

"Maybe we should go after them," said Jake, a strong drive of jealousy beating aside his fear. "It shouldn't be *him* in there with her. It should be me!"

"Are you crazy?" shouted Elton. "We need to stop this, not join in."

Britta sat down again, whispering into Travis's ear. "Why don't we leave, too. We could go upstairs…"

Travis felt an urge to agree, to leave the table and go upstairs and make love to Britta. No, not *make love*. Fuck. It was that simple. That animal. But a part of him rebelled, a slightly tarnished morality shouting to be heard above the rush of hormones. This wasn't right. *None* of this was right.

"It's in our heads," he said suddenly, letting go of Britta's hand. He had no idea where the conviction came from, but he trusted it. "Whatever's going on has got into our heads. It's making us act this way. Resist it!"

"Why should we resist it?" said Jake. "What's wrong with a bit of bestial rutting!"

"Listen to the way you're speaking," said Elton, siding with Travis. "It's not you. Something else is speaking through you, making you act the way you're acting."

"Fight against it," said Travis, looking at Britta with a mixture of longing and worry. "You have to fight it."

Britta felt the rightness in what Travis and Elton were saying, but it was hard to deny the urges she felt. She wanted to rip off her clothes and take Travis there and then, in front of Jake and Elton. Why should she care who watched?

Because it's wrong, said a voice straining to be heard in her head. *Because it's not how you would behave. It's not how you want Travis. He's more than just a fuck to you.*

"You're right," she said, feeling some of the urges recede as her true feelings for Travis overwhelmed them.

"There's something very weird happening here."

Elton, meanwhile, had taken Jake in his arms and was holding him tightly, preventing him from leaving the room and going after Alison and Scott. "Snap out of it, Jake," he said, barely holding back tears. "I can't bear to see you this way."

Slowly, Jake's lust-filled eyes began to clear and his muscles relaxed. He no longer tried to escape from Elton's embrace.

"I think we've beaten it," said Travis cautiously. "Now we have to do something about Alison and Scott."

He was about to stand when the table exploded, the centre ripping apart, spinning splinters of wood in all directions. All four of those still around the table were flung backwards. Britta slammed into the wall. Travis tumbled off his chair, hitting his head as he did so. Jake and Elton were lifted off their feet and thrown into a corner. The table upended, a jagged hole in the middle.

Blackness oozed from the floor where it had stood, spreading rapidly. Stygian blackness.

The table shuddered, slid, and then tumbled into the black hole, disappearing in an instant, leaving no trace.

Travis, stunned and bleeding, stared fearfully at the blackness edging towards his foot. This was what Dennis had seen, he was certain.

The surface of the blackness, where he had not previously seen any surface, rippled, bubbled, and something rose from beneath. A ragged, angular something, streaming with blackness that ran like oil. Raggedness that slowly coalesced in his mind to torn clothing. Angularity that became bones and joints, some with flesh, others without. And atop all this, breaking the surface with grim, grisly clarity, a face, with holes in its cheeks, missing an eye, hair ripped from a bloody scalp. Travis did not hesitate in his recognition.

"Swan!"

As he spoke the name, the body sank, more rapidly than it had surfaced, the blackness closing over it until there was no ripple, no sign, no *surface* anymore.

He was still staring into that infinite depth of darkness when two eyes snapped open within, and he heard Britta scream.

CHAPTER TWENTY-FIVE

Frank Grimes, the owner of The Deep Anchor, happily married with three children, fucked Kath Raymond with crazed abandon. He could not control, nor resist, the overwhelming urge that swept upon him as the young barmaid headed into the store room, throwing him a teasing smile as she did so. He had followed, found she was already lying on the small table, her panties thrown in a white puddle on the floor, her skirt around her hips, legs open. Now, as he thrust again and again deep inside her, and she moaned and writhed and dragged sharp nails down his bare chest, he thought of his wife, Natalie, and his children, George, Wendy, and Nathan. He didn't want to do this, to be unfaithful with a girl half his age. But he couldn't stop. The urge, the desire, the *need* would not let him.

He cried as he orgasmed, barely noticing that Kath cried, too.

Inside the pub, the bar was in turmoil as the patrons indulged in unrestrained, wild, and out-of-character sex. The compulsion that swept over them was too strong, too dark and heavy to resist.

In the houses of the surrounding streets, reaching as far as Wyatt Road, people who had long lost the desire for carnal coupling did it in whatever room they happened to be at the time; husbands, wives, lovers, brothers, sisters… The urge was so powerful, it overcame all social and moral boundaries.

The nearby park echoed with the sounds of lust. The streets were empty save for several dogs, trailing leads, wondering why their owners had abandoned their walk and pushed them away.

CHAP+ER TWEN+Y-SIX

Simon stood in the rain on the street corner opposite The Deep Anchor. Britta had not been at the Travelodge, and she was not inside the pub. He had searched both locations thoroughly. Now he stood watching, staring wildly at every person who hurried through the rain.

Where was she? He had to find her. He was *impelled* to find her.

Some part of him still felt connected to the sliver of *Yggdrasil* he had returned. Not an intellectual connection, but an emotional one. A *psychic* one. He *felt* the divisions of the nine worlds, knew that he stood in *Midgard*, home to all humankind. And he knew that Ottmor Wood, despite its geographical closeness in purely human terms, lay in *Nifheim*, the world of fog and mist. Why else would they have discovered *Gjallarbru* there? Below *Nifheim* lay the home of the dead, *Helheim*, and *Gjallarbru* was the bridge that connected the worlds of the living and the dead.

It was where he must take Britta. When he found her.

He turned away from The Deep Anchor, feeling a quickening in the current of *Gioll*, rushing below *Gjallarbru*, and a tremble in the root of *Yggdrasil*. Something of import had begun nearby, and he was drawn back along the road towards Ottmor Wood, past it to the top of Wyatt Road. Great things were happening, and he was close to completing his part in them. He was close to Britta.

Scott had just found his rhythm when the crash of the exploding table dragged him from the hormone-flooded dream he had fallen into. He looked down at Alison, who lay naked from the waist down on the kitchen floor, her legs wrapped around his buttocks, and saw the same shocked, embarrassed, and frightened look in her eyes that he felt in his own head.

They separated quickly, without a word, and scrambled for their tossed clothes to cover their nakedness.

Alison knew she had instigated this situation, and the depth of her embarrassment and shame was a palpable pain in her stomach. She had no idea what to say, if anything could be said, and tried not to notice that Scott was still erect, just as she tried not to notice the ache in her loins that begged her to take him inside once more. It was unthinkable, and yet the desire was still there, albeit overshadowed by her rediscovered morality. Above all else, she felt confused.

The noise that had broken the spell on both of them was forgotten in the awkwardness of their silent dressing.

Scott struggled to find something to say. Something that would make Alison feel better and assuage his own guilt. But he could find nothing other than a ridiculous urge to tell her he had enjoyed it! He was horrified that he even considered such a thing.

The tense atmosphere in the kitchen was finally broken by Britta's scream. Without thinking, both Alison and Scott ran through the hallway, ignoring the open front door and stopping at the doorway into the front room.

They stared in open-mouthed horror at the black nothingness that almost filled the floor space. Travis, scrambling back from the expanding edge, was the closest, and they called out to him through the roar of swirling air that all but drowned out their voices.

Travis, turning at the sound of his name being called, took a moment to focus and recognise Alison and Scott in the doorway. After some hesitation, and another look into the baleful eyes in the depth of the blackness, he pushed unsteadily to his feet and reached out a hand towards Jake and Elton, who were pressed against the back wall of the room.

Jake was bleeding badly from a head wound, the blood running down his face and dripping from his chin. Elton had to help him stand. Together, they edged around the wall towards Travis, all the time staring fearfully at the darkness that was beginning to lap, wave-like, on the floor, each time crawling closer to the skirting board. With agonising slowness, they drew nearer to Travis's outstretched hand until, finally, Elton was able to grab hold and be pulled the last inches.

The surging wind increased its ferocity as the three friends huddled together, their toes almost in blackness, their eyes squinting against the dust and splinters twisting in the air around them.

With Alison wedged as firmly as she could manage in the doorway, Scott edged into the room, holding on to her outstretched hand with grim, sweaty fear. He got as close to the black hole as he dared, and reached out. Travis, Jake, and Elton shuffled closer to him, Travis testing the distance with his own arm every few seconds. A sudden hurricane-like gust staggered them, and Elton had to hold tighter to Jake to stop him tumbling into the nothingness. As it eased, they moved forward again. Travis reached out, almost touching Scott's fingertips. They moved again, and again Travis stretched out his arm. His fingers touched and grasped and, in one monumental effort from all of them together, Travis, Jake, and Elton were pulled from the room into the relative safety of the hallway.

All five struggled to catch their breaths. Alison checked on Elton, who thankfully did not mention her earlier behaviour, and the two of them helped Jake to the stairs. They sat him down and examined his head wound.

"It's not as bad as it looks," said Alison with obvious relief. "A lot of blood, but nothing too serious. I can take care of it."

"Thank you," said Elton, smiling at his sister. "It's nice to have you back."

Alison blushed and tried to hide it in her examination of Jake's head.

Jake said nothing, still stunned and a little confused from his injury.

"Where's Britta?" said Travis in sudden panic, turning back and forth as though he expected her to miraculously appear.

"Did she...?" Scott pointed towards the still-growing blackness, now almost completely covering the front room floor, but Travis shook his head.

"I would have seen it happen. I was looking in that direction all the time."

"We heard her scream," said Scott. "So where did she disappear to?"

Travis, turning again, stared for a moment at the open front door. "Who opened that?" he said, looking from Scott to Alison.

Both shook their heads.

"It was open when we came out of the kitchen," said Alison, trying hard not to sound awkward or embarrassed about what they had been doing in there.

"She must have got away and run outside," said Scott as he and Travis hurried to the door to check.

There was no sign of her.

"I need to look for her," said Travis. "I have to find her."

"I'll come, too," said Scott.

Elton looked at the two in the doorway, and then to his sister.

"I can look after Jake on my own," said Alison.

"I have to help them," Elton said, lifting Jake's head gently so he could look into his glazed eyes. "You get better," he said. Then, after a moment's hesitation, he leaned forward and kissed Jake softly on the lips. "I love you, you idiot."

Alison sighed theatrically as her younger brother stood. "I did wonder," she said. "Congratulations on finally coming out."

"Hell of a time to do it, though," said Travis, stepping forward and giving Elton a warm, genuine hug. "All the same, I'm happy for you. I might even stop teasing you about not having a girlfriend!"

Elton managed a smile despite his worry over Jake and the nerves that screamed in his head. It had taken him a long time to accept his true nature and the depth of his feelings for Jake, and now Alison, Travis, and Scott knew, too. Whether Jake would remember anything was doubtful, but he didn't mind that. He had said it, out loud, and that was the most important thing.

"This is all very touching," said Scott, standing by the door "But we need to be going after Britta. She could be anywhere out there. Anything could be happening to her."

Without another word, Travis and Elton joined Scott, and all three hurried out into the night in search of Britta.

Simon dragged the unconscious Britta into Ottmor Wood. He had to shift his grip again and again as blood from Britta's head wound covered his hands, making them slippery. It was regrettable that he had to knock her out, but a struggling Britta would have been more than he could handle. He had witnessed her strength on several digs and had no wish for it to be turned against him.

A howling wind rose as he entered the trees, whipping the branches back and forth, stirring fallen leaves within whirls of dust and debris. Thick trunks creaked, smaller ones began to bend under the onslaught of the increasing gale. Simon would have feared for his life, but he felt protected by the Norse gods that guided him. No harm would come to him, or to Britta. They wanted Britta, and he was their chosen servant to fetch her.

The creaks and moans in the wood took on the intonation of speech, although he could discern no words. It didn't matter. The gods were around him, and he did their bidding. Britta needed to be brought to *Gjallarbru* and to the root of *Yggdrasil.* They awaited her on the far side of the river *Gioll*, the dead of *Helheim.* It was no longer mythology; it was his reality. It would become Britta's, too.

"I have a theory," said Scott as he, Travis, and Elton ran out onto Wyatt Road. "But it's a bit wild."

"I think we're past the point of worrying whether things make sense," said Travis. "What happened in there made no sense at all. Can you see her?"

Down at the far end of the road, Ottmor Wood was being driven into a fury by strong winds that rapidly pushed towards them. Looking towards the top end, all was quiet, peaceful even. Whatever direction they looked, they could see no sign of Britta.

"Given where she's been working," said Elton. "I would suggest the wood is the obvious place to start."

The rushing wind hit them full on, a wave of gusting, spinning madness that rocked them on their heels. Above them, a thick, dark cloud that ran with the wind blocked out all moonlight, deepening the gloom around them.

All three men turned their faces into the onslaught and hurried towards Ottmor Wood.

"Tell us this wild theory then," said Travis as they struggled against the wind. "But make it quick in case Britta's in trouble. I hope you can talk on the move."

"Something ties all this to Jake and Elton's find

and our dig," said Scott, his words whipped away almost before Travis and Elton could hear them. He raised his voice to compensate, shouting against the roar of the wind. "There's more to this than mythology. Professor Forrester felt it, too, I'm sure."

"My belief is suitably suspended," shouted Travis. "Go on."

"Jake and Elton found a rock that claimed to be the bridge to the underworld."

"*Gjallarbru*," said Elton. "Crossing the river *Gioll* to *Helheim*." He shrugged as Travis turned surprised eyes on him. "I Googled it once we knew what the writing said."

"Yes," said Scott. "And I did a bit of research myself. This place only became known as Anbal after centuries of bastardisation, word-of-mouth errors, and simplification. The original Norse name was *andi-balkr*, meaning spirit wall."

"Lots of places 'round here have Norse origins behind their names," said Travis.

"Yes, but think about it."

They reached the stile into Ottmor Wood and hesitated as Scott continued.

"We have a place called spirit wall surrounding the entrance to Norse hell. This whole place is like a prison, holding in the dead."

"You're saying that when you, Britta, and the Professor began digging…"

"We opened up the entrance to Helheim," said Scott. "Everything up to now has just been the teaser trailer to the main event."

A cry from within the wood, barely heard over the roaring of the wind and the incessant creaking and groaning of the trees, had Travis's stomach twisting in knots.

He was certain he recognised the voice. He *knew* it was Britta.

As Travis hurried ahead, followed closely by Scott, Elton could not rid his mind of what he had done. He had admitted his sexuality in front of his sister, his friends. Even Jake, though he doubted Jake knew anything about it. He had *come out*. And he had admitted his feelings for Jake.

He and Jake had been friends long before matters of sexuality appeared to muddy his emotions. When they first met in junior school, they had found so many things in common—from TV to films to books, even their opinions on school meals and the not-much-better alternative of cold lunches prepared by their mothers—that they had naturally become friends. A short time after that, they were *best* friends, a connection they maintained with their move into secondary education. In their mid to late teens, they had found another common love in alcohol and weed, and it seemed to Elton that nothing could separate them. Then came girls.

Elton had tried, really tried, to fit in. To be Jake's *wing-man*, accompanying him to wherever Jake's current crush was expected to be. They had even double dated, with the almost obligatory stop in the park on the way home for a brief kiss and fumble. The girls had been willing, and Elton had tried his hardest to engage in the adolescent touching and groping, but he had no enthusiasm for the pursuit, and, in time, the girls noticed that he failed to get excited by their ministrations. Word got around, things were said, insinuated, and he became the target of bullying by the alpha-male types in the school. But Jake had always stood by him. Elton didn't need defending; he was quite capable of defending himself, but Jake had always been there at this side. And when the inevitable fights came, it was the two of them against the rest of the school.

Neither of them was exceptionally tough, and they frequently got the shit kicked out of them, but they always gave back as much as they took, and they never backed down. In time, that reputation overshadowed everything else, and they were left alone, which was how they liked it.

Somewhere in among all that turmoil, Elton had begun discovering things about himself. He didn't dislike girls—far from it—but they didn't excite him sexually. Nothing did, particularly. The oversexed teenage hormones had passed him by, and he wasn't sorry about that. What did excite him, emotionally, was being with Jake. He felt such an outpouring of affection for Jake that, at times, it scared him. About this time, he also discovered he wasn't completely asexual, as he had thought. There were people on TV, in film, in magazines, that interested him purely physically, and he did indulge in the odd fantasy. That they were all men had, at first, scared him. What would other people say if they knew? What would Jake say?

An increasing acceptance in mainstream media, ignoring the rabid outpourings of parts of the tabloid press, and the sheer magnitude of gay pride processions in nearby Liverpool, finally brought him to the realisation that what he felt was perfectly normal, and something he could happily accept about himself. He was gay, and there was nothing wrong with that at all; in fact, it felt wonderful.

With one exception.

He could not risk Jake finding out. Along with the acceptance of his sexuality had come the realisation that he loved Jake, but he was afraid that if Jake knew, it would destroy their friendship. He would rather suffer the occasional pain of unrequited love than the permanent separation from his best friend.

It was an extra worry that he could have done without as he hurried to catch up with the others. His sole focus had to be on finding Britta. Everything else, even Jake, needed to be put aside. For now.

CHAPTER TWENTY-SEVEN

As she struggled back to pain-filled consciousness, Britta's first impression was one of confusion.

What was happening? Where was she? Someone was holding her, dragging her, but who?

The last thing she remembered was the chaos of the seance, the black hole eating up the floor, and the sudden force that slammed her backwards. She hit her head. She remembered the crack, the pain. The rest of the memory was muddled by her semi-conscious state, dizziness, nausea.

Simon!

She had seen Simon entering the room, the strangest smile on his face. Quite unlike anything she had ever seen from him before. He reached for her. To save her.

No!

Something in his hand. He swung. Another crack stabbing through her brain, and then nothing.

All of the thoughts, the memories, the reasoning,

took less than a second, and she suddenly knew who was dragging her through the undergrowth, with trees creaking and crying all around her in a gale-force wind.

Simon!

She began to struggle, to twist and turn, reaching backwards, searching for his face with her nails, ready to gouge deep, bloody lines in any flesh she could find.

He's gone insane. I'm not sure what he's up to, but something's snapped.

She screamed at him to let her go, but his grip held strong. His knee drove into her back, and she cried out in pain. His face leaned into view above her, but before she could strike, his head powered downward, thudding into her nose. She felt something crack, blood spurting from her nostrils, over her lips. She tasted iron in her mouth as the trees began to spin around her.

The strengthening wind only vaguely registered in her barely conscious mind. It roared like a speeding train, tugging at her clothes, her hair. Her struggles were weak and largely ignored by the professor she had once so admired.

She thought she recognised her surroundings, a stirring of recent memories fighting through the haze. It was the dig in the woods. Why had he brought her to the dig?

Further reasoning was curtailed by the sudden release of his hold. She slumped backwards onto the ground, the agony in her head jarring, flashing hot pain through her brain. She struggled to stay conscious, afraid of what Simon might do to her should she lose the ability to resist. But the rising darkness in her head was too strong, and although she fought it, her eyes closed, her brain ceased to interpret outside stimulus, and she succumbed.

Travis led the rush into the woods and towards the scream. Somewhere ahead of him Britta was in trouble. He had no thought other than saving her. Not even the cruel whip of branches, nor the uneven ground, could slow him. He knew Elton and Scott followed, but he would not wait for them.

The dig. For whatever reason and through whatever power, the dig was where Britta was.

The increasing head-on storm caused him to struggle and lean into it. Grit and dirt peppered his face, stung his eyes, but he kept on. Nothing could be allowed to delay him.

Through tear-smeared vision, he saw the clearing in the trees, someone he thought might be Britta's professor standing there. And on the ground, still and helpless, was Britta.

He needed no more data to form a rushed, but fortunately accurate, conclusion.

Travis ran screaming into the clearing, launching himself at the professor. The two men clattered to the ground, rolling, scrambling unceremoniously at each other.

Simon fought with the rage and power of the insane, uncaring about his own pain. Travis defended and fought back almost as furiously. There was no subtlety, no rules in the confrontation. Fists, elbows, knees, heads, all clashed and bled.

Elton joined the fray, pounding on the professor. Scott stayed back, unsure what to do. Confused. He had known the professor longer than any of these others, except Britta. What should he make of Simon's apparent abduction of Britta? Whose side should he be on?

Elton succeeded in dragging Simon away from Travis, holding him down as Travis climbed wearily to his feet.

"What have you done to her?" demanded Travis angrily through deep, gasping breaths.

"It's not me that wants her." Simon sneered, no longer struggling. "She's wanted by the gods. She's called by Hel."

"Hell?" said Travis, looking over to the prone form of Britta, wanting to run to her but needing to know what had happened. "What are you talking about?"

"*Hel*," said Scott, stepping forward, deliberately not looking at his professor. "One 'L.' The Queen of the Norse Land of the Dead. I told you. This whole thing revolves around Norse mythology in some way."

Simon laughed. "It's not mythology. It's reality."

"Whatever it is, it's over," said Travis, barely containing his anger. "We're calling an ambulance, and the police."

"You're too late," hissed Simon as the storm grew wilder about them, threatening to push them off their feet.

Dark movement, seen from the corner of his eye, turned Travis towards the hole dug by the archaeologists. The blackness within was roiling, breaking over the edge, flowing like thick molasses along shallow channels in the woodland ground. He could do nothing as it spread beneath the still unconscious Britta, widening until...

"No!"

Travis threw himself towards Britta as she began to slide into the blackness. He reached for her, stretching every muscle, every fibre he could. She seemed so far away, so out of reach! His fingers brushed her foot, and he grabbed, barely gaining a hold on her toes. It was too weak a grip to maintain for long. He could already feel her slipping. He didn't have enough purchase to pull. He could either let her go or be pulled into the blackness with her.

He had decided he couldn't let her die alone when firm hands grabbed his lower legs.

"Move up to a better grip," shouted Elton from behind him. "I've got you."

Travis pulled himself forward, straining everything to move quickly. He risked releasing his hold on her toes, immediately grabbing further up, breathing a sigh of relief as he closed his fist around her ankle.

With Elton pulling from behind, Travis edged backwards, dragging the still unconscious Britta with him. He almost had her clear of the creeping blackness when Simon, in a wild rage, rushed in and began stomping on his hand.

"You cannot deny the gods their prize!" he shouted, phlegm spitting into the still-rising wind. "She belongs to them!"

Travis cried out as the professor's boot crashed down repeatedly on his fingers. He could feel his grip on Britta's ankle weakening. Something snapped and a sharp pain stabbed from his hand up his arm. He couldn't fight back, and neither could Elton. If either let go, Britta would disappear into the hole. All he could do was try and withstand the agony and hold on!

When the stamping stopped, Travis was momentarily confused. His hand still throbbed, but there were no new blows coming down. Why?

The debris lifted into the air by the wind almost blinded him, stinging his eyes as he tried to look upwards. He could see the vague shadows and outlines of two figures, struggling. After a moment, he saw it was the professor and Scott.

Scott had pulled the professor off, dragging him away from Travis. But the professor fought back with mad abandon. Scott staggered under wild, swinging blows. It looked likely that the boot would be back before long.

"Pull!" shouted Travis, hoping Elton could hear him above the roaring storm. "Pull while we've got the chance."

He felt Elton pulling him back, and he held on to Britta's ankle despite the hot pain burning in his hand. Slowly, he was pulling her clear of the blackness. But even as he did, it seemed to be reaching out to her, crawling ever closer.

He risked a look towards where the professor and Scott had been fighting, but he now only saw one figure. And as it stepped closer, he could see it was Professor Simon Forrester.

It was hopeless. It was too soon to risk standing, to risk letting go of Britta's ankle. There was nothing he could do. Elton's grip on his legs tightened, and he guessed that he, too, had seen the professor returning for another attack.

Scott loomed out of the flying dirt and broken branches in a final, desperate lunge. He slammed into the professor, both of them tumbling to the ground and rolling dangerously close to the encroaching blackness.

The professor held on to Scott's left boot as his own feet slipped into the widening hole. The eyes he turned on his student held no pleading, only rage and madness.

Scott lifted his right foot and slammed the heel

down onto the professor's fingers, crushing them between the two boots.

With a cry of sudden pain, Simon released his hold, and Scott, in one final show of contempt for the man he once so admired, kicked out, hitting the professor squarely in the face.

The professor rolled, unable to stop himself as whatever lay in the blackness grabbed hold and pulled.

Simon Forrester sank into the blackness with one final scream of rage, of venom. Then he was gone.

After a moment's pause, Scott hurried to help Travis and Elton, and between them, they pulled Britta to safety.

"Thank you," said Travis. "If you hadn't grabbed the professor..."

"I should have helped sooner," said Scott. "But it was so difficult, accepting that he was no longer the Simon Forrester I knew and admired. Something had got into him, taken him over."

"I think it's trying to take everything over," said Travis. "That stuff is spreading!"

The blackness oozed from the hole, devouring grass and weed, a cancerous growth clawing up the trunks of the closest trees.

"We need to get back to Jake and Alison," said a weak, trembling voice from behind them.

Travis turned to look at the physically and emotionally drained Elton.

"You saved me," said Travis. "If you hadn't grabbed my legs when you did..."

"It's what friends do," said Elton. "But like I said, we should get back."

"You're right," said Travis, trying to hold at bay the trembling he felt rising throughout his body. Exertion, adrenaline, and the relief in being alive, and in Britta being alive, combined to drain him. But he forced himself to his feet and, with Elton's help, lifted Britta between them.

Behind them, the blackness continued to spread, unstoppable and hungry.

CHAPTER TWENTY-EIGHT

Frank Grimes stepped out of The Deep Anchor, naked from the waist down, his underpants trailing from one ankle. In a blank-faced daze, he shuffled into the street. The irresistible pull, the desire, the *need* to answer the call, smothered all other thoughts, other considerations. He had to obey. He *wanted* to obey.

Behind him came the waitress, Kath, her clothes in disarray. And behind her, Frank's wife and children.

From other exits, the patrons of the pub staggered out, slack-jawed and vacant-eyed. They all gathered beneath the old pub sign, rusted hinges creaking and squeaking in an ever-strengthening wind. As their destination became clear in their minds, they moved as one in the direction of Ottmor Wood.

More people came from houses, the park, the shops. Alison's boss, and recent crush, Edgar Leonard, moved with the crowd, followed by his wife and children. His business partner, Harry Ford, and Ford's daughter, Jean, were close behind. But there was no recognition in their eyes, no acknowledgement of the close friendship between them. They shuffled forward, like bad actors in a zombie movie, mindless of all but the call. Unseeing of anything, save their ultimate destination.

Deeper within the wood, those who lived closer had reached the first probing fingers of the slow-moving Stygian blackness. Without hesitation, they walked on, dragged beneath a surface that remained placid and flat, into a nothingness that had no limit to its hunger or depth.

Frank Grimes waited his turn quietly, in a bizarre line that snaked back through the trees, onto the road, and into the village centre. Even stripped of all conscious control, the population of Anbal formed a quintessential, and orderly, English queue. When his time came, Frank stepped forward and was gone, without even a glance back to his recent lover, or his family.

They followed close behind.

The Leonards and the Fords were carried, unresisting, along with the crowd.

There were no cries of fear, no attempts to run. Anbal committed mass suicide in an eerie silence, disturbed only by the shuffling feet through the fallen leaves and twigs that littered the ground of their approach.

CHAPTER TWENTY-NINE

"Can someone explain to me what the fuck is going on?" Elton asked as he pushed past another shuffling, vaguely familiar resident of Wyatt Road.

"It's pulling them in," said Scott. "*Helheim*. Feeding on them."

"We can't achieve anything by trying to stop them here," said Travis, grim-faced and pragmatic. "We need to regroup at Dennis's house. Then we might find some way to help."

Moving quickly up Wyatt Road, weaving through the entranced walkers, Britta slowly regained consciousness. She began to support some of her own weight, feet shuffling, then stepping.

Elton, eager to get back to Jake, moved away, quickening his pace.

"Simon…" said Britta, a little hoarse, her mouth lined with dust and dirt from the wind-blown wood.

"He's gone," said Travis. "I'll explain everything later.

But now we need to get back to the house. Can you walk?"

"I'll do my best."

She noticed, for the first time, the stream of people pushing past them, heading into the wood. "What's wrong with them? Why aren't *we* like that?"

"Doesn't matter," said Travis. "We're *not* affected, so we have to try and *stop* it instead!"

⟨⚡⟩ ⟨⚡⟩ ⟨⚡⟩

"I've the strangest feeling I've missed something massively important," said Jake, his eyes slowly clearing and the world gradually taking on a recognisable form.

"You mean apart from exploding tables, a hole in the floor that almost sucked everyone down into it, Britta disappearing... Apart from them?" Alison carefully checked Jake's head wound. It was scabbing over and healing well.

"I remember all that, except the bit about Britta." Jake slurred his words slightly, his tongue feeling strangely alien in his mouth. Too big. Too dry. "Maybe Britta disappearing was the thing I missed. Is that where the others have gone?"

Alison hurried into the kitchen, trying not to look at the floor where she and Scott had behaved like animals in heat. That was another Alison, a wild, *possessed* other. She would never behave that way. Never.

"Are you okay?"

Jake's voice dragged her back to the present, and she realised she had frozen in place, before the kitchen sink.

"Yes. Fine."

She half-filled the glass she found upended on the

173

draining board with tap water and hurried back to the hallway, relieved to be away from the worrisome, disturbing memories.

Jake took the drink with a shaking hand. His tongue became human again as he drank, and he felt able to talk with more clarity. "It wasn't your fault," he said, softly. "It wasn't you. Something else was in control. We all felt it."

The smile that twitched the corner of Alison's mouth had little humour in it. "You remember that, too," she said. "I was hoping you didn't."

"It doesn't matter," said Jake. "It's not important. But you still haven't answered my question about the others."

"The others," she said. "Yes, they went to find Britta."

"And Elton was okay going with them?"

"He volunteered. He…" She hesitated. Should she say anything to Jake? Was it her place to do that?

No, she decided. *It's something Elton should do himself, if…*when *he gets back.*

"He *what*?" said Jake, curious. "What were you going to say?"

"Just that he wanted to help," said Alison, thinking quickly. "He wanted to help find Britta."

"Well, he better come back safely, the idiot." Jake shook his head, wincing as his wound stabbed sharp pain through his skull. "Without me there to protect him, anything could happen."

He turned to look towards the living room door and the blackness that still lapped at the edge of the hall carpet. "Why has it stopped there, do you think? Why hasn't it come out here and swallowed us up?"

Alison said nothing. She had no answer to give.

"I'm sure there's something sentient in there," said

Jake slowly, fighting back the headache that began to pound harder, faster. "Either inside or... perhaps the blackness itself is sentient?"

"How do you mean?"

"It's a bit vague," said Jake, closing his eyes, trying to remember. "I'm no medium, but something reached out and communicated with me. Just before all hell broke loose. Something in that blackness, or the blackness itself, tried to talk to me. I'm sure of it."

For a moment they sat in silence, Alison watching Jake, and Jake staring at the blackness, his brow creased in concentration.

"What are you thinking?" said Alison.

"I'm thinking there might be some good in trying to communicate again."

"You're crazy," said Alison, shocked. "That thing tried to kill us all."

"Some part of it did, yes," said Jake. "But I wonder if there's more to it than that. I wonder if there's something else in there. Something less aggressive. Maybe it can help."

"And if you're wrong?"

Jake shrugged. "In the long run, I don't think we have anything to lose. Eventually, it'll break out of there and flood the house, maybe the world. This way we have a chance to learn more about it, and maybe even stop it."

With only the slightest hesitation, Alison nodded her agreement.

Jake began to shuffle forward, towards the blackness that waited in the doorway. He stopped. In a rare moment of decisiveness, fuelled by the belief he may soon be dead, he turned, leaned back towards Alison, and kissed her.

She took a shocked moment to respond, but then her mouth opened and they kissed with a genuine and long-suppressed passion. When they separated, they were both gasping for breath.

"I don't care that you're Elton's sister," said Jake. "I've wanted to do that for ages!"

Smiling, Alison watched as Jake once again shuffled slowly towards the blackness. Tight balls of anxiety sat heavy in her chest, her stomach, her whole being. Jake had to come out of this alive. He just had to.

Jake could still feel the fluttering in his stomach from making the bold move to kiss Alison. But it had been totally worth it. At least if he died following his stupid idea, he would die reasonably happy.

As he reached the doorway, he could see that the blackness not only lapped at the walls of the room, it crawled up them as well. Dark tentacles writhed towards the picture rail. The plaster cracked, infected, and fell away in brittle sheets. The bricks of the exterior wall began to crumble as the darkness soaked into them. On all the walls, splits and holes appeared, solid mass dissolving away. The blackness consumed the room. Perhaps it would consume the whole house? The only place so far untouched was the hallway. He didn't understand why, but given that both he and Alison were there, he wasn't complaining.

As he watched, the outer wall fell away, and the blackness oozed out into the garden. Spider-web tendrils crawled over the picture rail and spread across the ceiling.

If there was a way that communicating might stop this thing, he had to try. But he had no idea *how* to communicate with it. Should he *think* his call? Should he say it out loud? He could do nothing other than follow his instinct—and not the one that told him to run away.

He tentatively reached out a shaking hand and lowered it towards the blackness just inside the door frame. When he touched, it was icy cold, and he pulled his hand back in an automatic, shocked reaction. He tried again, this time prepared for the intense chill. He stopped with his hand floating on the blackness, feeling as though he had thrust his hand into a freezer and pressed it to the inner wall. Already, there were stabbing pains in his fingers and thumb as the cold sliced into them. He knew he could not maintain contact for long.

"Is there..." He had been about to say *is there anybody there* when he thought how stupid and hackneyed that sounded. "Is there someone there who wants to help us?" He knew his voice shook, but he felt no shame in that. Anyone would be frightened doing this. "Is there someone there who tried to talk to us before?"

He jumped as hands landed on his shoulders, only to see Alison lean over, a strained smile beneath frightened eyes.

"I wanted to be with you," she said. "You don't mind?"

He shook his head. In truth, he was grateful for the support and felt it strengthen his voice.

"We need your help," he said, staring into the blackness. "We really need some help."

Both he and Alison screamed as a hand burst out of the blackness and gripped Jake's wrist in a tight and freezing fist.

Travis heard the screams as they approached Dennis's house.

Not waiting to see if the others followed, he sprinted, faltering only slightly at the sight of the partly demolished house. Bursting into the hallway, he shuddered to a sudden stop.

On the floor before him, Alison was struggling to hold on to Jake, who, in turn, struggled against the pull of a hand reaching up from the hole in the living room, a hand that ran with the blackness, streaked and stained with its passing.

"Jake!"

Elton shoved his way past Travis, joining his sister in trying to pull Jake back from the abyss. After a further moment's hesitation, Travis joined them.

Unable to find any clear space around the already desperate, grasping hands of Alison and Elton, he decided to take a greater risk and attack the hand emerging from the blackness.

The skin was slimy, the runnels of darkness viscous, but not wet. He tried for the fingers, growling at the pain that stabbed through his damaged hand, but the grip was far too strong for him to prise them away from Jake's wrist. Defeated, he grasped the arm itself and pulled upwards, trying to ignore his own agony. If Jake could not be pulled away from this *thing*, then the *thing* would just have to come up to them.

Jake was slipping into unconsciousness, his eyes glazing, his body unresisting as he was tugged back and forth. The prolonged contact with whatever lay in the blackness had drained all will, all awareness, from him.

Elton cried as he held on to Jake with a lover's determination. Alison's face was set in grim concentration.

Travis knew he could not let his friends down,

regardless of how much pain he was in.

His hands slipped on the arm, the enveloping slime difficult to get a solid grip on, but he kept trying. Trickles of freezing darkness ran over his fingers, and he growled at the stabbing pains they brought with them. But he would not give up, any more than Alison or Elton were about to give up. He thought that Scott was standing somewhere in the hallway of the house, but he was irrelevant. He had chosen not to engage with the strange ensemble rescue attempt. Britta stood nearby, still too weak to do anything other than watch and hope.

For a lengthy, slow minute, nothing seemed to give. A static image of bravery and determination. Then Travis saw movement. Jake began to lean backwards, and Travis could feel the *thing* beginning to rise, even with his frozen fingers.

He did not lessen his grip, rather dug in and pulled harder. He could see the smile on Elton's face, the growing relief on Alison's. Jake was still unresponsive, but each second pulled him further to safety.

Still, the hand gripped Jake's wrist, pulling more of the *thing* with it as Jake's friends won the tug-of-war.

The thick, viscous surface of the blackness bulged near the arm, a stretched blister that popped and ran as the *thing's* head broke the surface. Darkness streamed off the slowly rising visage, like black blood, dripping from the eyebrows, the nose, the chin, thinning hair sodden with it.

Travis stared. It was impossible, and yet he recognised the face. There could be no mistake.

"Dennis!"

Dennis opened his eyes, staring in near madness. His mouth fell open, blackness pouring from it as he roared. It was a roar of desperation, of pleading. "Swan's dead!" he said, his voice strangely liquid, bubbling. "*Fjǫrlvor* ate her and spat out her bones."

Stunned, Travis could do nothing but stare at this travesty of his friend. He was aware of Britta close behind him, and Scott a little further off. Alison and Elton clung on to Jake, unsure whether this apparition of Dennis would drag him down or leave him be.

Dennis bobbed suddenly in the blackness, as though tugged from beneath. His stare became more desperate, more pleading. "I only have a moment," he said, more liquid filth tumbling over his bottom lip as he spoke. "I had to tell you that Swan is dead, and so am I. You can't help us. But as it eats, you combine. As you die, you understand."

"Dennis," said Travis, finding his voice and speaking through tears. "What can I do? How can I help?"

Another tug from beneath, and Dennis's head momentarily disappeared beneath the thick surface, only to break through once more, intense pain evident through the viscous covering of his face. "Burn the root," he screamed, part agony, part desperation. "Burn…"

He let go of Jake, slipped free of Travis's grip, and was pulled violently into the blackness.

The surface smoothed quickly over, and Travis could only stare at where his friend had been.

"What did he mean?" he said quietly. "What root?"

Britta and Scott exchanged a quick glance.

"We know," said Britta.

CHAPTER THIRTY

They headed for Anbal from the top of Wyatt Road, crossing to the far side as they passed Ottmor Wood. There was no longer a shuffling mob melting into the trees. They had gone. Everyone had gone!

The storm still raged, trees creaking, some beginning to bend. The wind swirled about Travis and the others, never seeming to settle on one direction, always shifting, changing. They would lean into a head-on blast of cold air, then stumble as they were pushed from behind, or the sides. It was only a mile into the village, but it was set to seem much further.

The last Travis had seen of 20 Wyatt Road, it had been collapsing, rotten with crawling darkness. There was no going back there. Dennis and Swan were gone. Dead. But Dennis had given them one hope, one chance that would, perhaps, put a stop to this madness. He didn't have time to grieve. That could come later. For now, he and the others had a job to do.

Behind them, they had left an ever-widening lake of blackness, slowly eating up the neighbouring properties, the gardens, the road. In time, it would threaten the whole area surrounding Anbal, perhaps the whole of the Wirral, or the country. Travis refused to consider beyond that. It became too large a disaster to comprehend in terms of what began with Dennis hearing voices.

He hurried to the head of the small group, with Britta alongside him. She held his damaged hand, now wrapped in bandages found in the kitchen drawer at Dennis's, and assured him she was all right, although still aching and nauseated. Alison, Jake, and Elton were a short distance behind, and bringing up the rear, Scott, who was focused more on the smartphone in his hand than on walking.

Jake fell back, still feeling a little dazed from the blow to his head, but alert and capable. "Who ya gonna call?"

Scott, surprised at the sudden voice, looked up and took a moment to orient himself. He smiled, more with politeness than amusement. "I'm doing more research. Forrester may have been crazy at the end, but he knew his subject. He was convinced of a Norse connection to all this."

"You really think there's something in that?"

"I don't know," said Scott. "But if there is, it might help us stop what's happening. Also, that thing in the black stuff…"

"Dennis."

"…right, Dennis. He mentioned a name. *Fjǫrlvor*."

"Really?" Jake laughed, a brief and humourless laugh. "I thought he was just speaking gibberish."

Scott read from the text on his phone. "*Fjǫrlvor* is a guardian of the gateway to *Helheim*. In our terms, a demon. Filled with lust and rage, it manipulates the sexual urges of others," Scott blushed slightly at this, "and pulls them under its control."

He stopped reading and looked up at Jake, his face pale, the blush gone beneath the pallor of fear.

"And it has an insatiable hunger for human flesh!"

The village centre was deserted. Window displays were lit, shop doors open, but no people served or queued. An eerie silence lay shroud-like over everything, dampening even the roar of the wind.

"This is just weird," said Elton. "Even on a Sunday the place has more life than this."

"Everyone was drawn to the hole," said Britta.

"Are they dead?" It was Alison who asked the question many of them were thinking.

"I guess so," said Travis. "If what Dennis said about Swan and himself was true, then the whole of Anbal has probably gone the same way."

Britta shuddered. "No survivors."

"Except us," said Elton. "Which means it's our job to kill whatever that thing is and close the hole."

"It's a demon." Jake caught up with the group, Scott close behind. "That name that Dennis used, Fjor... Fjudge..."

"*Fjǫrlvor*," said Scott.

"Yeah, that. It's a demon guardian, so Scott tells me. And it likes to eat people."

There was a sudden rising of the wind, whipping away the shroud of silence, screaming through the narrow main street of Anbal. It slammed shop doors shut, rattled windows, and staggered the small group of friends as they turned their backs to the fury.

"You think it's pissed we know its name?" Travis had to raise his voice against the roar of the storm.

"I don't think it was in a particularly good mood to start with," said Jake, making the others smile.

"We know what we need to do." Britta's hair whipped around her face, sodden strands clinging to her cheek, the bridge of her nose, her forehead. "Burn the root!"

For a moment everyone was silent, as though the storm had ripped the words from their mouths, battered the thoughts from their heads. They struggled to stand against the shoving and tugging of the wind. Near horizontal rain stabbed sharp pinpricks against exposed skin. Flying debris skipped past them, scarring the road surface. Most of it was unrecognisable, ripped from larger objects and thrown into the village. But then a garden ornament would tumble through, scattering shrapnel with each strike of the ground, and Travis winced as a hubcap span dangerously close to Scott's legs. An empty wheelie bin clattered clumsily along the pavement, its lid flapping like the mouth of some strange, ungainly beast. Before long, someone would get hurt.

Travis had fallen, unwillingly, into the role of leader within the group, and with that leadership came a responsibility to try and keep them safe for as long as he could.

"This way!" He gestured for the others to follow as he headed further into the village centre.

Between the Café QuietTime, one of the panes of its tinted glass frontage already cracked, and the old Pentecostal Church, there was an alleyway. The sides of the buildings gave them some relief from the onslaught of the wind as they hurried into it, out of breath and afraid.

"It's all very well saying burn the root," said Scott as they all caught their breaths. "But how?"

Even though the wind streamed through the alley, it was at a reduced ferocity, something they could endure after the full-strength rage. The rain continued to strike, but mostly as it ricocheted off the building walls. It no longer stung. Here they could stand, breathe, and talk with only slightly raised voices, rather than shouting.

"My lighter won't do," said Elton. "We need something that will keep burning, despite the wind and the rain."

Travis was hurriedly scanning the uncertain and incomplete map of the village centre in his head. There had to be something to help them, somewhere. When he found the answer, his only surprise was that no one, including himself, had thought of it earlier. "Anyone need petrol?"

Anbal Service Station was tucked away on Bik's Hill, a short one-way street that took traffic from Greasby and Irby up into the village centre. It was a small, unassuming shop, with two ageing petrol pumps and, off to the side, one diesel. Both the shop and the pumps had seen better days and people would often drive by without realising it was open. It always had a look of emptiness, of desertion, about it, only this time it truly was.

As they turned onto Bik's Hill, the friends no longer had the protection of the alley walls. The sudden strength of the wind surging up the narrow one-way channel made them stagger a few steps backwards. Showers of grit stung their eyes, peppered their faces, but, determined, they leaned into the angry gusts and struggled onward.

There was some small relief as they stepped onto the petrol-stained forecourt, set back from the street, affording shelter from the worst of the storm.

"Anyone know how to get the pumps going behind the counter?" said Travis, wiping his wet, gritty hand over his equally wet, gritty face.

"I do," said Scott. "I took a part-time job at a petrol station when I started university. Help pay the bills and buy food."

"Really?" said Britta. "I never knew that. All this time knowing you, but I never knew that."

Scott shrugged. "It didn't seem important."

"It wasn't," said Travis, snapping with impatience at the small talk and the easy camaraderie between the two students. "But it is now. So, you go and get that sorted while we get some stuff off the shelves."

Britta turned and glared at Travis.

"Look, I'm sorry," he said. "But we're kind of in a hurry here, and you two chatting about part-time jobs…"

"There was no need to get so grumpy about it. Surely you're not jealous?"

Travis was rescued from having to answer by Alison.

"As entertaining as it might be, listening to this little lovers' spat, can we stop wasting time and get on with whatever it is you want us to do?"

Travis felt burning in his cheeks, despite the wind and rain, and turned to the others. They were waiting for instructions from him and seemed to have some faith that he knew what he was doing. He had an idea, but that's all it was. He held no certainty that it would work. "We need empty bottles," he said. "Wine, beer, anything. Grab them off the shelves and pour them out on the floor. Some scraps of cloth, too. There must be some kind of cleaning cloths in the household section. And matches, lighters. We can't rely on Elton's all the time."

"You're making Molotov cocktails?" said Scott.

"That's the idea, but I've never done it before so..."

"Get some motor oil as well. A mix of petrol and motor oil works well, and only fill the bottles about two-thirds up."

"How do you know all that?"

Scott held up his smartphone. "Internet."

They found what they needed on the shelves and in the stock room at the back. With Scott activating the pumps, they filled thirty bottles with the combustible mixture, stuffing rags and cleaning cloths through the opening at the top, and leaving a liberal length hanging outside. The bottles were doled out and placed in carrier bags found behind the counter.

"Everyone okay with this?" shouted Travis as they prepared to re-enter the wind tunnel created by the walls that lined Bik's Hill.

There was a general nod of agreement, and they filed out, this time with the wind at their backs, pushing them onward.

The bags were not too heavy, but the clanking of the bottles, with each small swing of the arm, made them feel unsafe and liable to break.

"What do we do when we get there?" said Jake, letting the wind push him faster to catch up with Travis at the front.

"Light up these things and throw them at the root, or maybe the rock. More chance of the glass breaking," said Travis. "To be honest, I don't know any better than you, okay? I'm making this up as I go along."

"Hope this storm doesn't stop it from working."

"I'm pretty certain the rain won't put out a petrol

fire, but I guess we'll soon see."

They reached the alley with a collective sigh of re-lief. A slight respite from the storm while they headed back towards Ottmor Wood.

CHAP+ER THIR+Y-⊕NE

The blackness that had eaten Dennis's house flowed across the road, devouring tarmac, concrete, curbstone, and gardens. Lapped against the bricks of the houses opposite, undermining the foundations. It flowed speedily uphill, towards the main road to Anbal, but more slowly towards Ottmor Wood, hesitant, reluctant to trespass too soon on the events occurring within.

Had anyone been observing from above, via helicopter, satellite, or drone, they would have seen what appeared to be an enormous sinkhole, growing with each minute. But no one observed. The cataclysmic events happening in and around Anbal were overlooked by the monitoring systems within, and those focused on, the United Kingdom.

CHAP†ER THIR†Y-TW⊕

The first bolt of jagged lightning ripped through the dark sky somewhere behind the woods, followed quickly by a deep explosion of thunder that rattled the windows of nearby houses and brought Travis and the others to a sudden stop.

"That's got to be pretty much right above us," said Elton, moving almost imperceptibly closer to Jake.

"I don't like to be the one to bring this up," said Jake. "But, remember the dog walker?"

"And the dog," said Elton.

"What happens if lightning hits anywhere near these cocktails we're carrying?" said Scott, looking a little nervous, constantly glancing up towards the roiling clouds.

"You are a cheery bunch." Travis tried to smile through his own anxious glances skyward. "If it hits that close, I don't think you'll be around to worry about it."

Another tear of lightning, and a roll of thunder that grew and grew until Travis felt his insides shuddering. They only settled as the thunder faded.

"We need to get into those woods now," he said, no longer sure whether the itching trickles on his face were rain water or the sweat of fear. "That lightning will be right overhead very soon, and I don't want to think about where it might go to ground."

As they moved forward once more, battling the wind, blinking away the driving rain, Britta kept her voice low, speaking only for Travis to hear. "We're going under trees in a bad thunderstorm. Does that really make any sense?"

"Do we really have any choice?" Travis tried to smile at her, but the attempt was weak and his mouth would not turn upwards. "If we don't destroy this thing now, before it escapes completely into our world, we'll be dead anyway. It's got to be worth a try."

Travis saw Britta nod slightly before he turned his concentration to just putting one foot in front of the other, hampered by the wind and his own near-crippling fear.

He could only presume that the others were still following behind him and Britta. He was worried that if he slowed or stopped to turn back and check, he would never be able to move forward again. Only the steady, monotonous step by step prevented his fear from taking control.

The prospect of entering the wood, of confronting a creature that could entice a whole village of people to step into *Hel* and be devoured, made his legs weak and his mind rebel. Stubbornness and anger at the deaths of so many, including his best friend Dennis, were the only things that kept him moving. He didn't know what motivated the others, but he hoped it was powerful enough to prevent them from turning and running. Would the

Molotov cocktails work? Did they have enough? Why the hell were they going to stand under trees with a lightning storm directly overhead?

The last questioning thought was followed by the brightest flash of lightning yet, a white-hot rip in the clouds. The simultaneous crack and boom of thunder smothered the sound of the centuries old yew tree near the entrance to the woods splitting down the middle as though made of balsa. Thick, leaf-encumbered branches, collateral damage from the central destruction, clattered into the road, forming a sharp, snagging barrier every bit as effective as barbed wire.

"Ever get the feeling that someone doesn't want us coming any closer?" said Jake as he felt hands searching for his. He held them, Alison with one hand, Elton with the other.

"Don't suppose anyone thought to bring a chainsaw?" said Travis. He didn't wait for the obvious answer. "Then I guess we try to move it."

Travis, Britta, and Scott moved to one end, Jake, Elton, and Alison to the other. They struggled to find firm handholds, slipping their arms through gaps in the jagged branches, trying to ignore the scratches across the back of their hands, the tugging and tearing of their sleeves.

After a count of three, they lifted. The branch was heavier than they had expected, but between them they managed to get it clear of the ground. Travis, Britta, and Scott held still, while Jake, Elton, and Alison moved their end around, away from the entrance to the woods. Each shuffled step was a struggle, branches scraping on the ground. Gusts of wind blew face-on into them, trying to push them away from their task, but they persevered, finally making a big enough gap for them all to get through.

With relief, they dropped the thick branch and, arms aching and scratches burning, picked up their bottles once again. Without a word, they hurried through the entrance into Ottmor Wood.

⚡ ⚡ ⚡

The cessation of rain as they stepped under the canopy of the trees was almost complete. The wind, too, dropped. Still blowing strong, howling and moaning through the trees, but not the hurricane strength they faced outside.

"This is weird," said Jake. "We've been here when it rains."

"Pretty much just comes straight through," said Elton. "Certainly doesn't stop you from getting soaked. And the wind is wrong, too."

"If anything, it should be stronger, not weaker," said Jake. "The paths through the wood usually channel the wind, making it worse, not better. This is so wrong."

As though to emphasise the point, a bolt of lightning stabbed through the canopy of trees, spitting dirt and debris their way, and delivering a blast-force like a punch in the chest.

Britta cried out and spun away, holding her hands to her face.

Travis hurried to her. Blood seeped between her fingers from a deep gouge in her left cheek.

"I'll be okay," she said. "It's not as bad as it looks. Just stings a little."

Jake turned, looked at Alison and Elton. Other than pieces of twig and leaf caught in their clothes, Alison's hair, and Elton's hat, they seemed untouched.

Jake sighed in relief. "This is getting more and more dangerous," he said.

"We're trying to stop a creature that eats people," said Elton. "Are you really surprised it's dangerous?"

Another lightning strike, deeper in the woods. They felt the impact jolt their insides and heard the crack, creak, and crushing as a tree fell somewhere up ahead.

"We need to keep moving," shouted Jake, and Travis nodded, his face creased with a frown of concern for Britta.

"I'm fine," she said, her hands dark crimson with blood. "And Jake's right. We need to finish this. Quickly."

As they began to move once more, Jake hesitated, turning back to Scott. "You need to put that thing away and keep up," he said.

Scott, once more studying his phone, looked up. "Sorry," he said. "But I think I might have found an explanation for how all this started."

"For now, we need to worry about finishing it. Tell us all later."

Scott, nodding, pushed the phone into his pocket and followed the others.

As they drew nearer to Jake and Elton's clearing, the ground beneath them began to shake, deep rumbles of subterranean thunder rolling under their feet.

"I don't mean to bring anyone down more than they already are," said Elton, "but I think things might have changed for the worse since we were here last."

"Wasn't that long ago," said Travis.

"There wasn't a storm going on under our feet then, either."

"Elton's right," said Jake, and Elton wanted to hug him there and then in the rain-swept, wind-blown woods. He held himself back, as he had done for most of the years they'd been friends. Always afraid of showing his true feelings, even now when he had declared his love for Jake to his sister, Alison. He wasn't sure if Jake knew, and he didn't want to risk their friendship, their closeness.

"You okay?" said Alison, moving to his side, both of them watching as Jake trudged further ahead towards Britta.

"Fine," he said. "Scared shitless, but fine."

"Just like the rest of us, then," said Alison, forcing a thin smile. "And in case you're wondering, I've not said anything to Jake. That's something he should find out from you, not someone else."

"Thank you," said Elton. "As sisters go, you're not too bad."

"However," said Alison. "I've no idea whether he heard anything while he was injured, and you came out to me. Sorry."

Elton shrugged. "If any of us live through this, I'll worry about it then."

Further conversation was abruptly curtailed as, up at the front of the group, Travis came to a sudden stop, and they heard his exclamation over the subdued roar of the wind and the clatter of rain on the leaves above.

"Fuck me!"

CHAPTER THIRTY-THREE

Travis was only vaguely aware that Alison and Elton had joined the others, who had gathered around him. He could feel Britta squeezing his hand in fear, but his own terror made it impossible for him to return the gesture. He was frozen, staring at the clearing before them.

The ground, which should have been sodden leaves in thick mud, was dotted with rippling puddles and pools of blackness, the same blackness that had eaten Dennis's house. Between, there was, indeed, mud. Black mud, almost as black as the puddles around it, with the sickening appearance of mucus, thick and shining. Scattered about were bones, human bones, recognisable vertebrae, scapulae, femurs, ribs, jaws, with and without teeth, and the splinters of shattered skulls. Thousands of bones, mixing with the mucus mud, a grotesque and sickening carpet, every bit as treacherous as the blackness within it. But the real horror of the sight before them was the rock, *Gjallarbru*, the bridge between the world they knew and *Hel*.

A tight spiral of screaming wind, dark with mud, surrounded the sandstone block. A narrow tornado that had ripped a path down through the overhanging trees, the broken branches of which tumbled within the column. The rock no longer stood on solid ground, but was surrounded by the largest pool of blackness in the clearing, its edges lapping at the mud and bones, threatening to grow wider. Broad, sturdy roots held the rock in place, disappearing down into the blackness, while others writhed, tentacle-like, in the air, thick and red, a rhythmic pulse running visibly along their lengths.

The final horror was not, at first, evident, skulking in the darkness and shadows beneath the rock, within the roots. But blazing, rage-filled eyes could not hide for long.

Travis recognized them. They had stared at him from the blackness in Dennis's house.

With a low, bowel-loosening roar, great muscled arms seven times the size of any human arm reached out from the shadows. Dark crimson scales glistened with a wetness that Travis feared was fresh blood. Great claws sought purchase in the mud and bones beyond the blackness. *Fjǫrlvor* was emerging, pulling itself from *Hel* into the real world, intent on spitting the bones of these intruders into the mud as it had so recently done the residents of Anbal.

"We're going to need a bigger bottle," said Jake, breaking through the debilitating shock that had frozen Travis and the others.

"Really?" said Travis in a whisper, half turning towards Jake. "Jokes, at a time like this?"

"When better?" said Jake. "And it worked. You were

completely mesmerised by that thing."

"Aren't you scared?"

"Terrified, as my dry-cleaning bill will show later."

Jake jumped as *Fjǫrlvor* let out another roar that shook the ground and turned his stomach. Its claws struggled to get enough grip in the mucus mud to pull its heavy body out from under the rock. And the blackness seemed to be trying to pull it back, running up over its scales, wrapping around its arms.

"*Fjǫrlvor*'s not meant to leave the entrance," said Scott, gasping, trying to catch his breath, teetering on the edge of a panic attack. "Its sole purpose is to defend *Hel*. A guardian, able to kill and devour those it entices in, but not allowed to abandon its post."

Travis stared at the pools of blackness with a suspicion that they were growing. He watched the writhing tentacle-roots, the vicious claws of the struggling *Fjǫrlvor*, the thick carpet of bones and mud.

"I wouldn't like to gamble my life on that," he said. "Plus, whether that thing can come out and get us or not, we still have to get in there and start a fire."

"Can't we just set it going here?" said Elton. "We've enough petrol to burn the whole wood down."

"We have to be certain we burn the roots," said Britta.

"You don't know that for sure," said Elton.

"I *believe* that."

"So do I," said Travis. "First, there was Dennis's house, and then the rock. The house is gone, we can't do anything about that, but those roots attached to that rock are significant. I don't claim to fully understand how, but, like Britta, I believe they are."

"Okay," said Elton. "So, who's got the best throwing arm?"

The obvious and simplistic answer was that they needed to hit the roots with their cocktails so they could guarantee they would burn. But first, thought Travis with dismay, they had to throw through the tentacle-like offshoots, and a very pissed off monster, either of which could prevent the bottle from reaching its destination. And then, even if they somehow hit the roots, he was not convinced the things were hard enough for the bottles to break.

"The only guaranteed way to get fires going is to hit the rock," he said, with more than a hint of despondency.

"Through that twister?" Elton shook his head doubtfully. "We won't get anywhere near the rock."

Alison, standing behind him, put a hand on his shoulder. "Whatever we're going to do, it better be quick. I'm not convinced that creature's sense of duty will keep it in there for much longer. And I don't want to be part of its next meal!"

A sudden change of wind. The tornado, swirling around the rock, lunged forward.

Elton staggered backwards, almost tripping over Alison, his eyes fixed on the spinning column of air and debris as it settled back to its almost sheer vertical position over the rock.

"That thing's fucking with us," he said, angrily biting off each word. "I swear it understands every word we say."

"Not going to argue with you on that," said Travis, also taking a few steps back from the maelstrom.

Britta stayed where she was, her eyes fixed on the rock, her look thoughtful.

"What is it?" said Travis. "You have an idea?"

"No," said Britta. "Sorry. But I have the strangest feeling I belong in there. I can feel it pulling me towards it."

Travis took Britta's hand and gently pulled her away from the edge of the clearing. She didn't resist, but her expression changed from thoughtful to almost disappointed.

Another change of wind, another lunge of the tornado, this time towards Travis and Britta. A sudden downpour of heavy rain clattered through the trees above them, bouncing off the bones that were spread across the clearing. It only lasted seconds, but it added to the group's already sodden aspect.

"A weatherman would have a breakdown in this place," said Jake.

Alison, shuffling from foot to foot, shivering, wet through, and chilled to the bone by the wind, stayed close to Jake and Elton.

"We have to do something soon, other than stand around talking about the English weather," she said. "Or I, for one, will die of hypothermia."

Travis began to arrange his Molotov cocktails on the ground by his feet. "We're just going to have to try," he said. "I can't think of anything else to do."

"And if the roots don't catch?" Britta, following Travis's example with her own bottles, voiced the doubt of them all.

"Then we're fucked. And, quite possibly, so is the whole world. Who knows where this shit will end?"

A heavy silence fell over them as they unpacked their only weapons. Despite the tornado, the rage of *Fjǫrlvor*, the sudden gusts of roaring wind, they heard nothing but their own doubts, their own fears, in their heads. Any bravado had long gone, as had all but the faintest glimmer of hope.

"This is ridiculous," said Jake, breaking the dark quiet. "We shouldn't be doing this! We're office workers, students, pot heads for Christ's sake. There should be police, or soldiers, with guns, grenades, flamethrowers!"

"I agree," said Travis, trying to stay calm, worried that Jake and others might be hitting their breaking point. "But they're not here, and we are. What choice do we have?"

"None," said Britta, picking up her first bottle. "We aim for the rock and hope it works."

Alison, without saying a word, bent and picked up a loose stone almost the size of her fist. She pulled her arm back and threw. They all ducked as the rock hit the edge of the tornado and spun off, violently ricocheting off a tree and disappearing in a pool of blackness nearby.

"It's really not going to work, is it?" said Alison, brushing dirt off her hands. "Just like you said, that tornado won't let anything through. Except *Fjǫrlvor.*"

"The creature?"

"Look at it," said Alison. "That thing is down among the roots, but I've seen it come forward, despite the wind. And those scales should be hard enough to break the glass. If we set *him* on fire, he could spread it back."

"Will he burn?" said Travis.

"Doesn't matter," said Elton, smiling at his sister, a look of pride on his face. "The petrol will burn, that's all we need."

"Just one problem," said Britta. "Look at it."

They turned and looked. *Fjǫrlvor,* as though it had heard and understood what they were planning, had shrunk back behind the roots, its burning eyes glaring out, showing no sign of venturing further.

"Shit!" Travis fell to his knees, despair finally overwhelming his body. "What chance do we have now? Our bottles won't get through the tornado, we know they won't. Alison had the best idea, but the thing's gone into hiding. We're fucked."

"Maybe not."

They turned to look at Scott, who had been back on his phone while the others had been discussing plans.

"I think I know a way to draw it out."

CHAPTER THIRTY-FOUR

Anbal village centre fell into the blackness. Streets, shops, the service station, The Deep Anchor, everything eaten by the ever-widening lake of destruction. Its edges lapped at both the Anbal and Wyatt Road entrances to Ottmor Wood, teasing the outermost trees with tendrils that burned and dissolved.

There was a storm surge that stretched the surface of the blackness, a convex swell that swept from Wyatt Road into Anbal, pushing the edges, finally, into the wood. And once the barrier was broken, the slow flood began.

CHAP+ER THIR+Y-FIVE

With the wind now thrashing around the tree tops and the roar of the spiral around the rock, Travis and the others were unaware of the new danger seeping, inexorably, towards them as they gathered around Scott.

"A while back," said Scott, addressing Travis directly. "You said that the maiden name of the first woman who disappeared was Bergelmir."

"Swanhilde Bergelmir," said Travis. "Yes. Everyone called her Swan."

"Well, in Norse mythology, Bergelmir was one of the frost giants, or Jotuns. When Odin and his brothers, Vili and Ve, killed Ymir, Bergelmir and his wife were the only Jotuns to survive. Most of the others drowned in Ymir's blood."

"You're not suggesting that Swan's parents…"

"No," interrupted Scott. "I'm not, but you must admit we now know there's more to the Norse myths than fairy stories. I can't believe it's a coincidence that the first person pulled into *Helheim* has Bergelmir as a surname."

"But how does that help us now?"

Scott turned his attention to Britta. "You said you felt an attraction, a pull, towards *Gjallarbru* just now."

Britta nodded, a little nervously.

"Britta is an old Norse name, right?"

"Yes," said Britta. "My father is English, but my mother's family originally came from Norway. Their surname was Hrungnir."

Scott quickly doubled checked his phone. "Another of the giants," he said. "No wonder you were so keen to come on this expedition. It can't be a coincidence."

"I agree," said Alison. "But how does it help us now?"

"Bergelmir was the first taken by *Fjǫrlvor*. Britta feels a pull towards the thing. Surely it's obvious that *Fjǫrlvor* will want a Hrungnir just as much as a Bergelmir? *Helheim* has opened, and *Fjǫrlvor* is picking off the last of the frost giants, or their descendants at least."

"And everyone else?" said Travis, taking a protective step towards Britta.

"Collateral damage."

"All of Anbal? Thousands of human beings, collateral damage?"

"*Fjǫrlvor* might have had specific targets in mind, but the thing will feed on anything within reach."

"I can draw it out," said Britta, her voice soft, low. "That's what you're suggesting, isn't it? If I stand out there, on my own, at the edge, *Fjǫrlvor* might be tempted out to get me."

"No way," said Travis. "It's too dangerous."

"Dangerous?" Britta smiled nervously. "It's nice that you're concerned, but if we do nothing, I'll be dead anyway. We all will. It's got to be worth the risk."

"But…"

"We'll all be waiting, just out of sight," said Scott. "When *Fjǫrlvor* comes out, we'll hit it with every Molotov cocktail we've got, sending it running back to the protection of the roots, taking the fire with it."

"It's the best plan we've got," said Jake. "I'm sorry, Travis, but it is."

Travis looked at the others. They seemed to understand his dilemma, his pain, but it was also obvious that they agreed with Scott.

"Travis," said Britta. "I don't mind. And you'll be there, ready to protect me when it comes for me, yes?"

Reluctantly, Travis nodded.

"Then let's do it," said Britta. "Right now."

Britta stood alone at the edge of the mud and bone-covered ground, making sure she didn't stand too close to any of the puddles of blackness scattered around. She said nothing, did nothing, other than stare at the tornado, the rock, and the roots beneath. Blazing eyes stared out, but she did not look directly into them. She feared that if she did, she would move towards *Fjǫrlvor* rather than the other way round.

She could feel the pull, a deep-rooted urge to step into the blackness, through *Gjallarbru*, and into *Hel*. Only her own strength, and the knowledge that Travis was close behind her, prevented her from moving. But that strength was weakening as the seconds passed. Something needed to happen soon, or she feared she would be unable to stop herself.

The eyes in the roots shifted, brightened, focused. Movement in the blackness, a disruption in the spinning wind, and *Fjǫrlvor* was rushing towards Britta faster than anyone had expected. A blur of dark scales, burning eyes, and roaring mouth caught them by surprise.

Britta staggered, almost fell.

Her friends hesitated, a moment of shock.

Travis was the first to regain his composure and react.

With a cry of anger and desperation, he ran from his hiding place, lighting and throwing his first cocktail in one quick movement.

The bottle smashed against *Fjǫrlvor*'s foot, the oil and petrol splashing over the scales, the fire taking hold.

Fjǫrlvor stumbled in his run, but his burning foot did not stop him.

Other blazing Molotov cocktails sailed through the air, some missing, some causing isolated fires on *Fjǫrlvor* that slowed him, but none caused a retreat as hoped.

The ground in front of Britta was ablaze, and she turned to run, to escape both the flames and the monster.

Fjǫrlvor leapt, claws outstretched.

Travis felt his stomach drop, his hopes die, as it became clear that *Fjǫrlvor* would reach Britta before he could. He didn't see Scott, moving quickly, with a burning cocktail in each hand.

As vicious claws scratched at Britta's back, dragging a scream from her and a ragged tear in her shirt, Scott was there, between *Fjǫrlvor* and Britta.

The creature could not ignore the immediate prey; it instinctively grabbed Scott, claws digging into skin, drawing blood and shrieks of pain.

Scott, despite the agony shooting through him as he was lifted from the ground, brought both burning bottles round in an arc, shattering them against *Fjǫrlvor*'s head. The burning oil and petrol burst across the creature's face, searing its eyes, spilling into its throat. Splashback hit Scott, and both he and *Fjǫrlvor* burned like grotesque, jerkily animated candles.

In panic, *Fjǫrlvor* dropped his burning prey and stumbled, screeching in pain, flapping uselessly at the flames, back to the supposed safety of the roots.

None of the group saw the culmination of Scott's plan as they tried to put out the fires that quickly consumed the young student.

Finally accepting the futility of their actions, Travis held Britta in a tight hug, trying not to think of how close he had come to losing her forever. Scott had saved her by sacrificing himself. And in doing so, he had ensured the success of his plan.

The roots were burning, tongues of flame flicking out around the rock. The tornado quickened, weaved, but could do nothing as the petrol stayed alight.

A blinding flash of lightning, striking down through the trees, temporarily seared everybody's vision to white. A shuddering underground explosion shook the ground and knocked any on their feet down to their knees.

Even before blurred sight gradually returned to Travis, he could feel the difference. While the roar of the storm had eased, the rain was now pouring through into the wood, soaking them as they tried to gather their senses. The wind, too, was blowing freely between the trees, though no longer of hurricane strength.

"*Gjallarbru* has closed."

Britta's voice, at his side. He reached for and found her hand. As his vision cleared, he understood what she meant.

The ground was still littered with bones in the mud,

but where there had been pools of blackness, there were now deep holes. No one seemed inclined to peer into one to find out how far down they went, but Travis felt confident they would be very deep indeed. The rock, with the inscribed legend "*Gjallarbrú*" was still there, but it now lay half buried in the ground. There was no hole beneath it, no sign of any roots, and definitely no sign of *Fjǫrlvor*. The gateway to *Hel* had, indeed, been closed.

The fires died, even those near the edge of the clearing and those that had consumed Scott's life. There were scorch marks, broken bottles, and half-burned rags scattered about, but otherwise nothing. No sign of the battle that had been fought there, save for the blackened body of Scott lying close by.

"He saved my life," said Britta.

Travis said nothing, but simply nodded. He felt guilty that he had not been the one to sacrifice himself for Britta, for the world. He felt guilty for all the bad feelings he had held towards Scott, fuelled by envy and jealousy. In the end, Scott had proved himself to be, quite possibly, the better man. And Travis felt guilty about that, too.

"We should get out of here and call someone," he said, climbing to his feet.

"That could be difficult," said Jake, who had walked a short distance into the trees towards Wyatt Road.

Travis, Britta, and the others quickly joined him, standing at the edge of a sharp drop into darkness. There seemed no bottom to the sinkhole that stretched before them, almost as far as they could see. Only a faint, misty suggestion of hills and trees on the horizon convinced Travis that the hole had not swallowed the rest of the Earth.

They spread out, edging cautiously through the trees, watching their feet. The sinkhole was on all sides of them. The clearing and small surrounding area of Ottmor Wood they were stranded on was an island in the centre of an apparently bottomless hole.

"What the hell do we do now?" said Elton, staying close to Jake who, in turn, stayed close to Alison.

Growing slowly through the wind and rain, they heard the sounds of sirens, police, ambulance, fire.

"Someone finally noticed this bloody big hole," said Alison, smiling.

Above, they could hear the rotors of a helicopter.

They were all smiling now, as much through relief as happiness.

Only Travis continued to seem wary. He looked back towards the rock, wondering. "Did we destroy it?" he said. "Has it gone forever?"

"You can't destroy *Helheim*," said Britta. "Whether myth or reality, it's always there in some fashion. Even under a different name, in a different culture, a different set of myths, it's there."

"But we stopped it spreading here."

"We stopped it," said Britta. "For now."

"Hopefully next time, it'll be someone else's problem. I think we've done our bit."

Travis and Britta stood, staring at the rock, the clearing, the bones. They looked at Scott and thought of the terrible cost paid by the whole of Anbal. So many dead.

They held hands and waited for the emergency services to arrive.

ABOUT THE AUTHOR

Neil Davies was born in 1959 and has found everything else to be an uphill struggle. He currently lives in the North West of England with his wife, two grown-up children and a cat. He divides his spare time between writing, painting and music. For more information please visit his official website - http://www.nwdavies.co.uk

The area the author lives in has a long Viking history, and many of the places mentioned in the story exist. Anbal does not exist, but similar villages do. If you live near one, you will recognize it.

And be sure to check out these other novellas from
Grinning Skull Press

A lost child.
A marriage shattered beyond repair?
John Baxter doesn't think so, which is why he has planned this weekend getaway with his wife. He expected a lot of shouting, a lot of tears, but in the end, he hoped to have a stronger foundation upon which they could start rebuilding what they had once had.
What he wasn't expecting was the home invasion...
...and the hell that awaited them beneath the rented cabin.

Death awaits you. Tim Ritter has just a few months left. At least that's what the doctors have told him.

But then he's been offered a second chance at life – and love. For a price. But is the price too high? The sacrifice too great?

Find out one man's answer to those questions in Dan Foley's Gypsy, now available in print and for Kindle, Nook, and Kobo e-readers.

THOMAS SMITH

MONSTERS

"I killed my parents when I was thirteen years old."

And now, with the murder of Missy Blake twenty-two years later, it's time for Jack Greene to finish what he started.

When the co-ed's mutilated body is found, the police are clueless, but Jack knows what killed the pretty college student; he's been hunting it for years. The hunt has been going on for too long, though, and Jack wants to end it, but he can't do it alone. The local police aren't equipped to handle the monster in their midst, so Jack recruits Major Kelly Langston, and together they set out to rid the world of this murdering creature once and for all.